Praise for

On *Baggage Check*:
"The author is so deft at crea___g ___eresting, 3D characters that I was instantly hooked into Sweetann's plight (yes, Sweetann). Even the bad guys have depth and lives beyond the story. This is not a typical thriller which makes it much more interesting than the average shoot 'em up, and Sweetann is not a typical heroine. A guaranteed fun time."
– Christina Lay, author of *Death is a Star*, editor at Shadow Spinners Books

On *How to Write a Sizzling Sex Scene*:
"All writers could benefit from reading this book, whether they're writing erotica or not. Fun to read and insightful. This book clearly shows how sex and sensuality can add zest and depth to any character's story."
—Alexis Duran, author of the Masters and Mages and Edges of Night erotic fantasy series

On *Black Leather*:
"A darkly seductive page-turner by a writer who knows how to put the erotic thrill into a thriller."
—*DarkEcho*

"An artfully written and highly recommended erotic and psychological suspense from first page to last."
—*Midwest Book Review*

On *Suspicions*:
"This is where she's at her best."

—*Locus*

"A spooky collection of tales."

—*Publishers Weekly*

On *York's Moon*:
"*York's Moon* is so absorbing and unusual that you'll almost miss how beautifully written it is—almost. Elizabeth Engstrom's mesmerizing and unique style will draw you into a world of mystery, violence and heroic struggle. Ultimately, this story celebrates the uplifting power of the human spirit. Do not miss it."
—Susan Wiggs, bestselling author of *Marrying Daisy Bellamy*

"With quirky, engaging characters, York's Moon is as much about understanding the human condition as solving a murder mystery. I cannot imagine anyone but Liz Engstrom writing this fine novel."
—Terry Brooks, author of the Shannara series

On *The Northwoods Chronicles*:
"A genre-blending exploration of love, aging, grief and sacrifice. Fast-paced, melancholy and beautiful, the overarching narrative binds a collection of good stories into a superb if unconventional novel."
—*Publishers Weekly*

"To read Elizabeth Engstrom is to be guided by the sure hand of an accomplished writer whose stories have the power to transfer readers to places both real and surreal. We believe in the unbelievable, marvel at worlds created between dream and reality, and reach for all that transcends the limits of our imagination."
—Gail Tsukiyama, author of *The Street of a Thousand Blossoms*

"From the ominous opening to the soaring conclusion, these braided stories – subtle and spooky and smart – will keep the reader spellbound.. The Northwoods is a scary place to live, but in Ms. Engstom's hands, it's a fabulous visit."
—Karen Joy Fowler, author of *The Jane Austen Book Club*

Books by Elizabeth Engstrom

Novels
When Darkness Loves Us
Black Ambrosia
Lizzie Borden
Lizard Wine
Black Leather
Candyland
The Northwoods Chronicles
York's Moon
Baggage Check
Benediction Denied

Collections of Short Fiction
Nightmare Flower
The Alchemy of Love
Suspicions

Nonfiction Books
Something Happened to Grandma
How to Write a Sizzling Sex Scene

Anthologies Edited
Word by Word (co-editor)
Imagination Fully Dilated (co-editor)
Imagination Fully Dilated vol. II (editor)
Dead on Demand (editor)
Pronto! Writings from Rome (co-editor)
Ship's Log: Writings at Sea (co-editor)
Lies and Limericks (co-editor)
Mota 9: Addiction (editor)

CANDYLAND

by Elizabeth Engstrom

IFD Publishing
P.O. Box 40776, Eugene
Oregon 97404 U.S.A.
www.ifdpublishing.com

This novel is a work of fiction. Names, characters, places and incidents are either the product of the author's imagination, or, if real, used fictitiously.

Cover art and book design by Alan M. Clark

First Printing: August 1998 in conjunction with TripleTree Publishing

ISBN: 978-0-9988466-2-0

Printed in the United States of America

CANDYLAND

by Elizabeth Engstrom

Eugene, Oregon

INTRODUCTION

The role of society in the development of the psyche has always fascinated me. Taking a situation to its extremes has fascinated the reading public, as most people are is interested in fantastic stories of children being raised by wolves or apes. We want to know how they adapt or fail to adapt after a certain point. But what about the other side? To what do we return when we retreat from society? What kind of ameliorating effect do societal mores have on our behavior? And to what extremes will damaged people go to make sense of it all?

This is the story of Peter and Tess, who took it to the limit. Perhaps we can all learn something from their experience.

—Elizabeth Engstrom
Eugene, Oregon

PROLOGUE

AUGUST

Tess surveyed the spoils of war that lay strewn in multicolored disarray on top of her new yellow satin bedspread. Boxes and bags, brightly colored and overflowing with silk, linen, leather and fur tumbled over each other and lay quietly.

Tess stood at the foot of the bed and watched the mound. She should be sliding the silks over her skin, twirling in the new fox coat, modeling for the mirror the lacy under things she'd never had the courage to buy. Instead, she just looked at them, and they looked garish, extravagant, stupid.

She reached over and plucked the little black velvet box from under the red chiffon cocktail dress, then cleared a corner of the bed and sat down. The knot in her stomach tightened as she remembered the buying frenzy, not two hours ago, when she had bought these diamonds with Charles's American Express card. She pulled the drawstring and the diamonds sparkled into her hand. They caught the last rays of sunlight coming through the bedroom window, and with each movement of her fingers, they shined and winked at her.

Diamonds didn't understand. They were too cold.

The diamonds rolled off her fingers, back into the bag. She looked again at all the merchandise on her bed. Supplies, she thought. Husband-catching supplies. Soon the divorce would be final, and Charles would take away his love, affection, status, security, and American Express gold card in return for a cash settlement.

She would be a divorcee. Used goods.

Damaged goods.

She would need these things, all these things and more, to help her find a new man, lock him in, get him to commit, get him to marry her, and then keep him.

An impossible task.

Dating again. Ugh. I'd almost rather be dead, she thought.

Tess gently slid down the satin bedspread to the floor, stockinged feet straight out in front, brown linen skirt wrinkling beneath. I will need these things, she thought, tears burning her throat. God knows, I will need something.

* * *

Peter listened to the telephone ring while he folded and refolded the bank statement along its worn creases. I'll answer it next time, he thought, and I'll tell him that I was out. That oughtta make him happy. He unfolded the paper one more time and looked at his balance. Unbelievable. It would have taken him years to win that much money on the pro tennis circuit. Instead, he did it in one day. In a civil court though, not on a tennis court.

But I would have had those years. I could have been one of the best, maybe even the best. Could have been. Could have been.

I could have been already too old, too.

The phone stopped ringing.

He folded the bank statement into a paper airplane and sailed it through the bedroom door into the living room.

Two o'clock. He fumbled the top off the aspirin bottle and spilled three into his hand.

Gently, he swung his bad leg from the bed and groped for his crutches. Wincing in anticipation of the pain that didn't come, Peter stood and made his way to the bathroom. He was healing. Actually, he was healed, but he didn't want to tell anybody. If they knew, they'd make him do something. Tennis had been his life. What would he do now?

Go out, his old man said fifty million times a day. Go out and coach. Go out and get a job with the tennis promoters. Go out and do something, anything. You're twenty-four years old, for Christ's sake. Don't just lie around.

Peter watched his reflection in the bathroom mirror as he swallowed the aspirin with a drink of water. He was too thin, too pale, too antsy, and taking aspirin out of habit.

Maybe the old man is right, he told his reflection. I oughtta go out, I oughtta get laid. He leaned on the sink, pressed his nose into the mirror. He watched his favorite illusion as his eyes merged into one, then he stepped back and noticed the greasy smudge his nose had left on the glass. He looked down at the dirty sink, and he smelled the bathroom, smelled the apartment, smelled his attitude. It stunk. It all stunk.

Maybe I'll hire a cleaning lady, he thought. And start spending a few of those dollars.

* * *

Arnie unlaced his work boots with one hand as he held the receiver to his ear with his other hand. He listened to Peter's phone ring over and over again in his ear. No answer. Again.

He sat on the sofa and pulled off his boots, his gut churning.

Peter was home, he just wasn't answering his phone. He didn't want to talk to his dad.

Arnie slammed the receiver into the cradle and put his head down into his hands. Give him time, the doctors said. He's had two major blows in one year. He'll snap out of it. He just needs time.

Well, he'd had enough time. Now it was time for that boy to get out and get busy. Someday he'd look back and see how he'd wasted his life. And by that time, it would be too late.

Arnie sat on the sofa and looked back. He saw how much time he himself had wasted. How much money. If he'd taken advantage of his time and money, he could have accomplished so much more.

He could have had more precious moments with Fran, opportunities he'd blown, opportunities he'd never have again.

Peter needs to understand about his opportunities.

That's what fathers are for, to teach their children about

their potentials.

All Arnie needed to do was figure out how to get Peter to appreciate all his future.

All Arnie needed to do was figure out how to get Peter to answer his phone.

DECEMBER

Tess felt the touch on her elbow, feather light, hesitant. Startled, she whipped around, feeling her red curls bounce against her forehead. A boy stood at her side, a young man really, closely trimmed blonde hair ruffled at the very front. His soft face registered surprise at the violence of her response, then he smiled, and she noticed the fullness of the lips, the fullness of cheek, the young innocence in his face.

"Wanna dance?" he asked, but the volume of voices, the background music and bar noise caught his words and swept them off on a wave of someone's cigarette smoke.

"What?" she said, knowing full well what he had asked, knowing, too, that she was too old, out of her element, overdressed and afraid.

He leaned close to her ear and she caught a whiff of his cologne. "Want to dance with me?" Then he pulled back and looked into her eyes.

Their eyes snapped together, and Tess fell into his trauma, seeing, deep within the blue, the pain, the hurt, the age that was far more advanced than his chronological years. She held onto that gaze with all of her strength, discovering life there, discovering death, discovering pain among people, and this boy had seen an equal share of it. She drank of his pain, she fed him her own, and as the need dissolved, the heat and the noise came up, and all that was left were two strangers facing each other in a loud and obnoxious bar.

He took her hand and led her gently off the bar stool, allowing automatically for her weak-kneed lack of strength, as if he felt it, too. She watched his slight limp as she followed him, finger hooked in his, brushing past young executives preening for young secretaries, toward the small dance floor, where couples moved slowly to Sinatra oldies. He turned, and settled his hands on her hips. A quick look at other couples showed her to place her wrists behind his neck, and she did, avoiding his gaze.

He began to sway, and pulled her hips tighter to him, and a hot knot arose behind her breastbone. To be small again, to be held in muscled arms, to be danced, romanced, flirted with, desired again. To be young and healthy and whole and in love.

She caught a ragged breath and pressed her forehead to his chest, smelling his scented perspiration, and she wanted to live this dance forever.

Sinatra blended into Johnny Mathis, and she felt his hands in her hair, then he bent his lips to her ear. "What's your name?" he whispered.

She pulled away and looked up at his face, surprised again at his youth, and said, "Tess."

He smiled, the little dots of perspiration on his upper lip stretching, and he said, "Tess. Tess. Tessa. Contessa." Then he pulled her head to his chest, and rubbed his thumb lightly over her cheek as they swayed, not moving their feet, merely absorbing each other's presence, and she heard her name in his chest as he whispered aloud, "Contessa."

The evening passed in fast fascination. Wet, sweaty glasses of cold, watery Scotch with melted ice followed wet, sweaty dances of hot, needful flesh pressed together, prolonging anticipation, prolonging agony. And then came last call, and he handed Tess her purse, then took her hand. She followed him out into the blast of December night air that forced a drunken shriek and giggle from her, and he looked at her with absolute love and tenderness in his eyes and hugged her close, warm, tender, with no musical accompaniment except that which played to the private audience of lovers.

She hadn't felt so young in—maybe ever. Maybe she had never been this young.

Holding hands and walking as close as her fox coat would allow, they walked up the darkened street, and into the warmth of an all-night liquor store. Tess stuffed her hands into the satin-lined pockets of her coat and watched with mild amusement as Peter purchased a bottle of Scotch, and she wandered toward the magazines out of courtesy as the greasy proprietor demanded his identification.

The cold air pounced on them as did a raging fit of giggles as they left the store and jaywalked to his brown Toyota. He opened her door like a gentleman, and she waited with fabulous amusement while he unlocked his side and got in. He handed her the brown-bagged bottle and leaned across for a kiss. She accepted both. It was a tender kiss, brief, light and loving, and after, they didn't move for a long moment, feeling the warmth of their lips, feeling the warmth of their faces so close together.

Peter pulled back then, and whooped, then fumbled his keys to the tune of her laughter and eventually they were on their way, heater blasting frigid air around their liquor-warmed bodies.

Charles would shit, Tess thought, and giggles bubbled up from her depths.

They kissed again in the elevator, and again in front of his apartment door, the warmth of their rapport becoming more intense, more eager, as they neared their destination. Tess felt giddy and free, she wanted to act out all the silliness she had ever seen in all the movies. She wanted to leave her shoes in the elevator, her coat in the hallway, her dress in the doorway.

This idea burst from her in a laugh that sent saliva spraying toward the wallpaper, and Peter pulled her close to him, laughing, saying "Shhhh." Then they both giggled until he could fit the key in the lock and manage the door open. He pushed on it and flicked on the light switch and said "Ta-da!" and Tess walked into his apartment, shedding her coat on the way.

"I'll fix us a drink," Peter said as he shut the door and locked it. Tess barely heard him. She was drunkenly transfixed by the living room wall, which was filled with pictures, plaques, trophies and certificates of accomplishment. Peter had played a lot of tennis.

She heard him rummage through ice cubes in the kitchen as she walked from one end to the other, reading the inscriptions, looking at the photographs of a handsome blonde boy in action, his whites stretched tight as he reached for the impossible backhand.

"Artifacts," he said, as he handed her a drink. "Artifacts from a previous lifetime."

"You were very good."

"Were. As in used to be. No more."

"What happened?" The Scotch slid smoothly down her throat.

"Hit by a car when I was crossing the street. How's that for a cliché? Drunk driver."

"Oh, Peter, I'm sorry."

"That's life, I guess." He rested his hand on her shoulder and toyed with her curls. She moved in closer, wanting to absorb his pain, hoping to leach it from him with a body compress.

"Want to see my scars?" His tone was mock-dirty-old-man, but Tess had fallen into alcohol-induced sadness at this young talent struck down in his prime, and she nodded, seriously.

He took her hand and led her to the bedroom, where they undressed each other with quiet tenderness, until she suddenly remembered. "Go turn out the light," she said, and pulled the spread from the bed. When he returned with their drinks, she was under the covers. Peter finished his in a gulp, then slid out of his shorts and slid in beside her. Tess felt his hands on her bare skin, felt him unhooking her bra, and she worried, for a brief instant, that he would notice her scar. Then she suddenly felt too close, too dizzy. She pushed him from her, thinking she would be sick, and as she did, the Scotch, the guilt and the excitement finally sapped the rest of her strength and with a sigh she lay back and passed out.

* * *

Gritty eyes cracked and a blast of light screamed into her skull. Her stomach rolled as her head pounded, her bladder was filled to capacity, and something thick clung to the corners of her mouth. As awareness increased, so did the sickness, and she fought her way from the tangles of limp sheet. One foot touched the carpet, then her hand, and she saw the shadow of her hair on the blue-striped bottom mattress. Her head began to clear, and panic would have set in, had she been any less sick.

Her stomach lurched and with an attendant burst of adrenalin, she kicked free of the covers and stood, the room reeling about her. Her unfastened bra hung down her front, and she pulled it off and let it fall as she staggered about the room, looking, increasingly frantic, for the bathroom.

She found it behind a door hung with maroon satin bathrobe and a hangar filled with striped ties. She pulled down her lacy panties and collapsed on the toilet, most of the sickness receding with the voiding of her bladder, and she began to relax, to think, to try to remember what had happened. She fingered the lace around her thighs. He hadn't taken advantage of her, that's for sure.

She ran fingernails across her scalp, feeling the headache

begin to pound anew. She wiped the goopy corners of her mouth on a square of toilet tissue before she wiped herself, and checked her panties again for evidence of foul play the night before.

They were clean. Then she flushed the toilet, stood and faced herself in the mirror.

Sick. Sick and pale, and mascara ringed her bloodshot eyes like some 30s Hollywood corpse. She stuck her tongue out, and it was coated and yellow. What a good time I had last night, she thought, then her mind began to actively ignore the hangover and deal with the problem at hand. She had brought no makeup with her, and she had no car in which to run home or down to the store, and she couldn't exactly remove her makeup and face him, him, the man in there, the man she had slept with...sort of...the man...Peter. She smiled slowly. Couldn't do anything quickly this morning, not even remember.

Peter.

She found his hairbrush and his toothbrush, and used them.

Feeling better all the time, she finally lathered up with some awful deodorant soap and washed her face, cringing at the damage she was doing to her tender facial cells. Finally, she stepped into the shower to wash off the clamminess.

When she was through, she found some skin cream for her elbows, knees, hands, and, with another cringe, she put some on her face. In the end, she felt fresher, but still kind of greasy, and definitely still hung over.

She wore the towel and looked quickly around the apartment.

It was small. Small kitchen, small living room, small bathroom, small bedroom. The living room was almost empty, a couch, a coffee table, a hanging plant, a circular rug on top of the green carpet. No books or magazines or anything to indicate that anybody had ever been in there. The kitchen was just as barren. She went back to the bedroom, where Peter still slept, his chin darkened with morning beard. The bed looked old, somehow, used, stinky, distasteful. She could lie on the couch in the living room, but it was too far away, too cold.

She pulled the top sheet over the bottom, and turned the pillow over. Still wrapped in the damp towel, she lay gingerly on the bed, her back to Peter, and she and her misery curled up at the very edge.

In a few moments, she was asleep.

*   *   *

"Good morning."

She brushed at the headache that skittered just out of reach.

"Tess? Are you awake?"

She opened her eyes to see Peter standing over her, showered and shaved, wearing a wet blue towel around his waist. He carried a tray. She brushed at her hair, pulled up the towel that barely covered her, rubbed her hands across her face, embarrassed that he should see her this way, but determined to make the best of it.

"Um-hum, I think so." She sat up and pulled the towel up again. Peter plumped her pillows up against the headboard and she scooted up, careful not to show either breast or pubic hair.

"Breakfast," he said, and laid a tray of scrambled eggs, sausage and buttered toast on her lap. The tray also held two frosty green bottles of Heineken beer.

"Oh, I don't think I'm very hungry," she said, but as the aroma drifted around the room, her stomach began to rumble. She sipped the beer. And again. Soon she was eating with ferocity, certain that nothing had ever tasted this good before. Peter fetched his plate from the kitchen, and they sat cross-legged on the bed, feasting.

"How did you happen to be at Mario's last night?" Peter asked, then sipped his beer.

"I was supposed to meet a friend, Carolyn, but she never showed up." Tess wiped toast from her lips and licked her fingers. "I was just ready to leave when you showed up." She sipped her beer. "What about you?"

"I don't know. Here." Peter got off the bed, opened his closet and pulled out a light blue dress shirt, then handed it over to her. "Put this on instead of that ugly towel. I won't look."

He turned his back and Tess shed the towel and donned the big shirt, rolling up the sleeves. She tossed her hair, felt the beer easing away the hangover, and said, "Okay."

He turned back toward her and appreciation shone in his eyes. "That's much better," he said. He sat back on the bed and toyed with his toast. "I've always dreamed of having a woman in my apartment who liked to wear my shirts... and who looked as good as you do in them. I never really believed—" He blushed and took a bite of his toast.

He looked so young, so vulnerable. Tess reached over and kissed him lightly on the cheek, then, feeling embarrassed herself, went back to her breakfast.

"So you're a tennis player who got injured. What now?"

Peter seemed relieved to have something else to discuss. "I don't know. That's what I've been asking myself. That's what my father calls and asks me ten times a day. He thinks I should

coach, or promote, or something, but somehow, tennis… It's just not—I just don't want to anymore."

Tess nodded, chewing slowly. She could understand how someone could be soured on something he used to love. She used to love Charles, and now she didn't want to think.... Oh. He was probably in front of the judge at this very moment, she thought with a jolt. Finalizing their divorce. She would be single before noon. She put down her fork, the headache threatened to return, the sickness began to slowly revolve around her, she thought she would lose her breakfast all over the bed.

"Tess? You all right?"

She looked up into Peter's young, fair face, a lad, really, who had adoration in his eyes, and the sickness receded.

"Just hungover, I guess."

"Yeah, me too. I'll get us each another Heinie."

When he returned with their beers, Tess had regained her composure. "How old are you, anyway?"

"Twenty-four. And you?"

"Thirty-four. Old."

"Not old. Perfect."

Tess smirked at him and drank half her beer down. It tasted wonderful. "When's your birthday?"

"August tenth."

"Really? Mine's August ninth."

"Both Leos. We'll have to celebrate."

"Celebrate. Yeah. Thirty-five. I'll celebrate with a face-lift, probably."

"There's nothing wrong with your face."

"No, it's just beginning to wrinkle."

"Character."

"Sure."

"I mean it," Peter said. "I think you're one of the most beautiful women I've ever met."

"Oh, Peter...." She was going to say what an old, worn out line that was, when she looked at him and realized he meant it. "Well, thanks. I feel like I'm old enough to be your mother."

"You're not."

Tess finished her beer and put the bottle on the tray and set the tray on the floor. She sat up on the bed, cross-legged, and stretched her head down to touch the bed. Then she stretched her arms out wide. "Thanks for the food, I feel a lot better now. I ought to be going."

"Where?"

"Home."

"Why?"

"Well, because it's got to be close to noon."

"So? What have you got lined up today? It's Thursday. If you worked, you'd be at work. So since you don't, is there some place else you'd rather be?"

Tess thought about her expensively furnished apartment: the closets of expensive clothes, the vanity filled with expensive cosmetics, the cold neatness in every room that was dust-free and never really lived-in. She used the apartment minimally, never really living there. There was no point, by herself. The furnishings were selected by the decorator and had never become her own; the apartment had been purchased by Charles without her participation—in fact his mistress, or his mistresses, as the case may be, probably lived there in succession before he pawned it off on her in the settlement. It was not really her place.

She looked around Peter's bedroom. It was a mess, but it was a fun mess. He lived here, all the things on the walls were of his own choosing, it smelled like him, it looked like him, and it was a fairly comfortable place to be. "No," she said. "I guess I don't have a reason to go home. Except..." and she pulled at the blue shirt that was all she wore over yesterday's panties.

"You don't need more clothes here. You look great, just the way you are."

Tess punched up a pillow and lay back, feeling sexy

for the first time in years. She crossed her long legs at the ankle, noticing they'd kept their Bermuda tan for almost two months—at least they looked tan next to the dingy sheets. "Peter, if I'm going to stay much longer, we have to do something about these sheets."

He jumped off the bed. "Great! Let's change them."

His enthusiasm was highly contagious. She got off the bed, too, feeling her panties show as she bent over. She didn't mind.

She pulled the old sheets off as Peter disappeared into the other room. He returned with a fresh set, but they looked little better than the ones they were taking off.

"These sheets are all gray!"

"They're old."

"You don't have any with flowers? Or, you know, those geometric patterns?" She took the fitted sheet from him and shook it open.

"No. Just white."

"We need to buy you new sheets. And a mattress pad."

They made up the bed and then got in, pulling the sheet up over them, sitting up, resting their backs on the pillows next to the wall. Peter drained his beer and reached to the nightstand for the television remote control. He switched it on.

"Soaps. I hate soaps," she said, watching him, feeling his body heat, his presence so close, yet he hadn't touched her. How intriguing. He seemed to want her there just because he wanted her there.

"General Hospital. It's my favorite."

"Yuck."

She, too, finished her beer, then snuggled down and watched him watch his program. I think I really like him, she thought, and that's a nice way to spend my first day as a single woman. She smiled to herself and softly fell asleep.

* * *

When the fabric softener commercial came on, Peter looked over at Tess. She was breathing slowly, her cheek flushed against the white of the pillowcase. Her red hair flounced about her face. She had that classic cute look. It was amazing. Freckles all over her little round nose, big blue eyes with black lashes and black eyebrows, curly red hair. She must have starred in a zillion cereal commercials when she was a kid. He could still see the child in her as she slept. She looked so peaceful, so innocent.

He met her in a bar. Was that how Arnie met Fran? How did they meet, anyway? Peter closed his eyes and pictured them on the screen of his mind's eye. Young. Innocent. Both of them in their early twenties. In college. They met in a malt shop, he decided. Just like on "Happy Days." That was their era. It was love at first sight, just like it had been with him and Tess. He could just see them, spotting each other across the crowded room full of be-boppers. The next day Arnie saw her studying in the library. He sat next to her, asked her out, and it was nothing but roses and perfect love from that moment on. It had to have been that way. Arnie and Fran only had eyes for each other. Their love was so perfect, so seamless, so solid. When Peter was born, he was born within their cocoon. When he turned pro and left home, he parted the strands carefully so as to not damage any. He could still go home and enjoy the warmth.

Then a doctor took both hands and ripped their cocoon wide open, jerked Fran out and left his father dancing, naked and cold in the light of the world.

But Peter had seen the love. He knew it existed. He could have it. He would have it. Tess could be the one. Tess was the one.

He looked up at the ceiling. "God," he whispered, "if you've sent her to me to make up for my bad hip, I'm grateful. In fact, if she'd stay with me, I'd gladly give up my other one.

Just please, God, don't let her go home."

Then he smoothed the curls away from her forehead, watched her poke one finely-formed leg out from under the sheet in her sleep, and went back to his daytime television.

When he woke up, early winter night had fallen. The clock read six-fifteen. Tess was still sleeping. He turned off the television, pulled the yellow blanket from the floor where it had fallen, and covered her, then snuggled up to her back. He began stroking her bare leg, fingers gliding gently under the band of her bikini panties, then over her hip, around the curve of her stomach, to touch one perfectly-formed breast with his fingertip.

The aching loneliness inside him expanded until he could barely breathe. This was the most wonderful woman he had ever known. He couldn't believe she was really, truly, here in bed with him. He'd had lots of girls before, tennis-circuit groupies, but they were gum-chewing, empty-headed twits, most of them. Not like Tess. Not like his Tess, his Contessa. God, he had to have her.

She stirred, moaned a little breathlessly, and he wasn't sure if she was still asleep or not, but she made no move to dissuade his advances, so he gently pulled her panties down to her knees, and cuddled up to her back and probed between her thighs. She moved to help him. She was moist and ready. He slipped in and came immediately, yet his penis remained hard. He rocked slowly, moving her with him, God, she was so sweet, and then he pulled out, turned her toward him, caught the panties with his toe and pulled them off, then slipped back inside her again. Her eyes were filled with the heat of desire, and he kissed her, gently, then unbuttoned the shirt she wore, kissed those magnificent breasts and tenderly sucked the right nipple until she began the climb to her climax.

They reached orgasm together, Tess hugging him so tightly he thought he would explode inside her, and when it was over, Tess cried. He held her and rocked her and brushed the hair from her sweaty forehead and kissed the tears from her cheeks.

"I've always felt like I was alone before," she whispered. "I guess I've never really made love with someone until now."

Peter held her and pulled the sheet and blanket over them and they slept, entwined.

* * *

"Peter, wake up."

Peter came instantly alert. Tess was sitting up in bed, her eyes wide open. "Peter, I have to go home."

He sat up and took her hand. Her eyes shone in the darkness. "Why?"

"I don't know...It just seems I've been away for a such long time, and suddenly I'm afraid."

"I'll go with you."

"No, that's okay...I'm...I'm all right."

"I don't want you to go. Please. Please don't leave me tonight."

"Peter...."

"Let's just sleep and tomorrow we'll go to your apartment and get what you need, okay?"

"It's not like I'm moving in here."

"Why not?"

"Well, because..."

"You don't like it here?"

"I do...."

"You don't like me?"

Her eyes closed, her face softened. "I do like you. I like you a lot. I like you more than maybe I should."

His spirits jumped, skipped and then thudded. "I don't understand."

"My divorce was final yesterday, and..."

"So that's all this was? A celebration whoopee? Pick up a guy in a bar in defiance?"

"No! Oh, no, no." Her soft hand touched his cheek.

"No, that's not it at all. No, I just don't feel like I'm ready for another relationship right now."

"Relationship. I hate that word."

She bowed her head, nodded, the irrepressible bounce of her hair glinting in the dimness. "Me, too."

"So let's never say it again. No relationship, no nonsense, no pictures, no "stuff," okay?" He saw the smile on her pert face as she looked up at him. "There's just you and me right now, here, in my apartment, in my bed, getting to know each other, falling in love, being real and true and honest moment by moment. Okay?"

She nodded.

"Good," he said, and his relief soared. "Then let's find something to eat."

She swung her legs off the bed.

"Wait."

"What?" she asked.

"Let's decide what to eat before we get up."

"Why?"

"So we don't waste time, that's why."

She settled back down. "What do you have?"

"Frozen pizza, peanut butter, bread and Heineken."

"Let's eat peanut-butter pizza and have a beer."

"Perfect." She was the one for him.

Peter turned on a light and pulled on a pair of pajama bottoms, Tess donned the blue shirt she'd been wearing, and he went to the kitchen while she went to the bathroom. He got the pizza out of the freezer, popped into the microwave, got out the peanut butter and two beers. He took the beers into the bedroom, put them on the nightstands. When Tess came out of the bathroom, he told her to spread the peanut butter on the pizza when it came out of the oven, and then he shut himself in the bathroom and stared into the mirror.

"I can't believe it," he whispered. "She's really staying with me. Good God, I love her." Then he relieved himself, washed his hands, noticed he needed a shower and a shave, and went back to the bedroom, where Tess sat, cross-legged in the center of the bed, pizza cutter at the ready, peanut butter pepperoni pizza in front of her. Oh God, he thought. She's just perfect for me.

He looked at the clock. "Six minutes," he said.

"Six minutes?"

"From bed to bed. Six minutes. I think we can do better than that."

"Pizza took four."

"We'll work on it."

She cut the pizza and they ate, without benefit of plates or napkins, then licked the peanut butter and pizza sauce off their fingers, then each other's fingers, then each other's cheeks, then lips, and soon they were delving into the pleasure of each other, at first wild and giggling, and then soft and tender.

This time they slept the rest of the night through, wrapped around each other.

In the morning, the telephone woke them.

Peter reached for it the way he always did, but his arm

was wrapped around Tess's shoulders, and the cobwebs that fuzzed his mind swept away with the sight of her, all puffy-faced and cuddly. He looked at the clock. Nine-ten.

The phone rang again.

Tess yawned, stretched.

The phone rang again.

"Aren't you going to answer it?"

Peter looked at her. One naked breast poked out from under the sheet. He wanted to kiss it. "It's my father."

"So?"

"So, I'd rather talk to you."

They snuggled and listened as the phone rang five more times, then stopped. The silence seemed like his father's presence in the room, more so than a distant telephone call. I should have answered it, he thought. I'll call him after breakfast.

"Peter, I have to go home today." She turned in his arms and lay one leg over his.

"I'll go with you. I have some errands to run, too."

"What?"

"New sheets. Food. We'll run errands, go to your place and then come back here. We can do it in an hour. Sixty minutes from bed to bed."

"No, we can't. I have to do some things at home."

"What?"

Tess pulled away from him, held the sheet tightly to her chest as she groped around for the blue dress shirt she'd worn the day before. "I don't know. Things. I need maybe to be alone for a while." It was under the bed. She put it on and began to button it.

"I'll drop you at home, go do the shopping, and then come back and pick you up. You can get your shampoo and jeans or whatever you think you need. Okay?"

She turned to face him. "I don't know, Peter. I've been here two nights already, without going home."

"So?"

"So, maybe that's not so good."

"It's been wonderful for me, and I think it's been very good for you." His heart began to pound. Please, God, he thought, please don't let her go away from me.

She smiled and his spirits soared. "It has been good, Peter, but...."

"But nothing. Tess. Look at me." She finished buttoning the shirt and turned back toward him. "This crazy accident ripped my future out from underneath me. I had all my hopes and dreams and future and livelihood—everything I had ever thought about doing or being or having, all had to do with being a tennis champion. And now that's over. I'm not going to do that again. I made a vow to myself that I would just take each day as it comes. I've got enough money that I won't ever have to worry, and I'm not going to get caught up in abstract ideas that mean little except heartache."

Tess looked at her hands. Peter took them in his. "I've never enjoyed myself as much with another person as this time I've had with you. I know you're a little bit uncomfortable, and I don't want to pressure you, but frankly, you're the best thing I've ever had, and I don't want to let you go back to...to whatever...whatever it is that hurt you, and that might hurt you again. What we have is good, Tess, let's just do it while we have it." He thought tears might choke him.

She slowly pulled her hands away from him, and shook her head. "There are things you don't know, Peter."

"Then tell me."

She shook her head again.

"Look at me, please."

She looked up, her eyes darting from one to the other of his, as if she was searching there for sincerity. Peter had never felt so sincere in his whole life. "Now tell me."

She took a ragged breath. "When you find out, you won't want me anymore."

"I can't imagine that."

She looked down again, and he saw the twinkle of a tear run down the side of her nose and make a dark spot on the sheet. "I can't have children," she said, then raised her eyes to him with a challenging look.

Peter almost laughed out loud, except he knew that would slice her far deeper than anything else. But what could he say? He felt such relief, he just took her in his arms and held her close. She began to sob.

"Tess, Tessa, my Contessa. I don't care about children."

She sniffed and pulled away from him, then wiped at her face. "Sure. You say that now. You're so young yet. But what if when we get older, you...."

"I'm not looking too far ahead, remember?"

She sniffed and nodded.

He plumped up the pillows and brought her back down with him, whipped the sheet up over them. "Children were never a part of my life's plan. I was going to be too busy being on the circuit to settle down and have a family until I was much, much older. I had decided that marriage was not for me, and therefore, children. I'd gone through the entire scenario, too, you know, bouncing the blonde little boy on my knee, watching him grow up and be a tennis champ, but I looked at my priorities and my goals and decided that I could do without that. And now you're here, and I think God must have brought you directly to me, because you can't have kids and I don't particularly want any."

"I thought everybody wanted kids."

"Not everybody."

"Charles, that's my husb—my ex-husband, he wanted kids. He really wanted kids. He wanted—he wants—lots and lots of kids."

"This Charles is not too bright a guy."

"Oh yes he is. He's a—"

"He let you go, and that wasn't too smart."

Tess cuddled up against him. They rested, quietly, for a moment.

"Don't you think your heart has been broken because of all the plans you had for the future?"

Tess nodded.

"Well then why don't we just take it a day at a time? Do this with me. We'll just spend today together, because I love having you here, okay?"

Tess smiled. She nodded. "New sheets?"

"New sheets," he said. "Here." He wadded up a fistful of sheet and handed it to her. "Blow your nose."

She looked at him in astonishment, then with a giggle, did as he told her.

Tess took the sheets to the washer while Peter took a shower. Then Peter cleaned up the dirty dishes while Tess showered. Hair still wet, they scampered into their clothes, Tess complaining about feeling foolish in her evening coat and expensive wool jersey dress she'd worn to Mario's the night they'd met, and together they went out into the bitter, smelly cold morning in the city.

They huddled close together.

Peter unlocked his car and they got in, then looked at each other with wide eyes. "It's different out here," he said. "It's ugly. Let's get this over with."

He drove aggressively through traffic to Tess's building, where he parked underground and they got out, hearing the echoes of their footsteps and the squeal of tires on smooth concrete. Peter put his arm around Tess who seemed small and frail, not strong and female, as she had in his apartment. They got in the elevator that smelled like cigar smoke, and Tess pushed button number eighteen.

Her apartment looked like something out of a movie set. All the colors were muted pastels, perfectly coordinated. The expanse of fawn carpeting and matching draperies left Peter cold.

He shivered and hugged himself. "This place isn't you," he said.

"I know."

"Let's go."

"Wait, I've got milk in the fridge and...."

"So what?"

"So if I leave it, it'll spoil."

"Okay. I'll throw out the milk. You get what you think you need, and let's go. I hate this place."

Peter peeked into the bedroom as Tess went in to her closet. It was cold, too, frilly with yellow satin. He went to the refrigerator. There was little in there. He poured the milk down the sink, then went back to the bedroom. Tess was packing a bag.

"What are you doing?"

"Getting some things. Underwear, jeans, toothbrush, makeup, moisturizer, sweatshirt, sneakers."

"This place looks like Charles, and I don't even know anything about him."

"I know."

Peter sat on the edge of the bed. He clenched his fists to will himself to sit still while Tess finished what she had to do.

He hated this place. It made his face burn. He didn't want her here, he didn't want her to look at these things of her past, he didn't want her to be influenced by all this stuff, he didn't want her to ever come back here again. He would make her past disappear if he could, have her all to himself, create all her memories only of their times together. He was afraid that his dingy apartment and crippled leg wouldn't be enough for her after a while. He was afraid she would be attracted to yellow satin bedspreads and color-coordinated spaces again, and he couldn't stand that, he just couldn't stand that.

His agitation parted for a moment in astonishment. There was something other than tennis for him. He could do something other than moan alone in his apartment. His father was right. Sort of. He just wanted Tess. He just wanted Tess. He loved her and that amazed him. And he desperately wanted her to love him.

Tess clicked the locks on her suitcase and said, "I guess that's all I'll need for a while."

Peter stood up, feeling weak in the knees. "Good. Let's go."

He took her suitcase, put his other arm around her and escorted her out the door. "Hey, got your checkbook?"

"Yes, why?"

"I've just got an idea, that's all. C'mon."

They ran, hand-in-hand, down the hall to the elevator.

Peter bounced up and down on the balls of his feet as they waited for the doors to open, and then fidgeted as they rode down together. Then they ran for the car. He threw the suitcase in the back, got in, started it up and they were off.

"That was fast," Tess said.

"I can't wait to get home."

"Me neither."

Peter set his jaw and headed for Penney's downtown.

He parked on the street and almost said, "Wait here," but

thought better of it. He didn't want her out of his sight.

"C'mon," he said, locked the car and pulled her into the store.

They went to the linen department and he scooped up six sets of all-cotton sheets. White. Tess giggled. "C'mon," he said, and pushed his way to the front of the line. "Cash," he told the clerk, and ignored her smile. He was increasingly fidgety and uncomfortable.

Sheets in the bag, they ran through the store, back to the car. Peter threw the bag in the back and took off, headed for the financial district. He parked again on the street, in front of a major bank. He turned in his seat. "This is where my business manager works. He pays all my bills. Telephone, rent, heat, charge cards, everything. I want him to pay yours, too."

"But I don't know how much...."

"Let him handle that. He'll invest all your money and pay your bills and all you have to do is tell him what your bills are and how much allowance you want. It's a great system. Okay?" He felt her darting eyes searching him for sincerity again, and he hated it. "Okay?"

"Okay. I guess."

"Good."

Filling out forms took about fifteen minutes. Peter paced as Tess worked, and when she was finished, he grabbed her hand and rushed her out of the building, down four flights of stairs and back to the car. He started it up and they drove back to his place. He parked, grabbed the sheets and her suitcase from the back seat and ran to the door. He held it open for her, she ran ahead and pushed the elevator button and they rubbed noses until it came. On his floor, they flew down the hall, he fumbled with the keys until the door opened, they dropped the suitcase and sheets on the floor in the foyer, stripped off their clothes and soon were holding each other, safe from harm, safe from the outside world, naked, on a plain, stained, blue-striped mattress.

"Please don't leave me," he murmured into her hair. "Don't ever leave me."

Then the telephone rang.

Ice crystals shot through Peter's body. He felt Tess pull away from him, and he pulled her closer, hugged her tightly.

"Aren't you going to answer it?"

"It's my dad."

"So?"

"So, I don't want to talk to him."

She pulled back and looked into his eyes. Her gloriously Irish-blue eyes searched his restlessly, but it wasn't with suspicion, he realized, it was with affection. "If you don't talk to him, he'll come over here."

She was right. Peter sat up, swung his legs over the side of the bed, took a deep breath and picked up the phone. "Hello?"

"Peter. How are you, son?"

"Good, Dad, good."

"Been out?"

"Yeah, I've...uh, I've been out making arrangements."

"Arrangements?"

"Yeah, I'm leaving for England tomorrow, I have a meeting with a promoter. There's a chance I can get on with him, do some promoting on the world-class level."

"Well. Well, I'm surprised. I'm surprised you didn't tell me you had this thing cooking, son."

"It's a contact I made a long time ago, Dad. It just came up." He turned and winked at Tess. She was curled on the bed, holding a pillow to her stomach.

"Well, good for you, boy, good for you. Will I get to see you before you go?"

"Not likely, but I don't think I'll be gone long. Maybe just a couple of days, then again, maybe a month. I've got everything on this end taken care of, though, and I'll be keeping in touch."

"Please do that, Peter. Call. Text. Email. Or even send a postcard. Goddamn, I'm proud of you, boy."

"Thanks, Dad," Peter said, and a knot began to form in his throat. "I've got to go now."

"Take good care. Give my regards to the Queen. And good luck!"

"Thanks. Bye."

Peter hung up. His dad just wanted him to do something with his life, and Peter's lie had made him proud. It was a stinking feeling. He put his head in his hands and scratched his scalp. Then he felt her feather touch on his back. He turned and saw the most beautiful woman on earth, naked, on his bed. "Hi," she said.

"Hi," he said.

"You okay?"

He nodded.

"Clean sheets," she said, and they jumped off the bed, ripped open a package of clean, white sheets and had the bed made and were back in it in less than two minutes.

"We're getting better," Tess said, and Peter loved her.

* * *

England! That could only mean Wimbledon. Arnie clapped his hands, then stood up and did a little dance. Good for Peter.

He felt mildly guilty that he'd been thinking Peter was doing nothing with his life but feeling sorry for himself, when in fact, he was still out making contacts in the tennis world. Arnie had been sure Peter hardly left his apartment. Well. Just goes to show, old man, that you aren't always right.

He sat down, clapped his hands again, grinning like a chessy-cat. He wished there was something to do to celebrate. He'd like to take Peter out for a celebration, but he was busy.

He looked around the living room. It was so quiet. The Saturday loneliness in the corners began to wake up and drift into the room.

"No," Arnie said. "No more. I will celebrate my son's success. I won't waste more time. I won't waste another weekend."

But he wasn't quick enough, and the loneliness grabbed at his ankles and then climbed up him and covered his head like a rubber sheet. "Fran," he whispered, sinking back into the couch, and he knew he was lost. Down for a long count.

* * *

Monday morning, Arnie woke up on the living room floor. He could hear his clock radio in the bedroom. The news was on. He rubbed his eyes and then sat up. All the family albums were open and strewn about the living room floor. All of the framed pictures of Fran and the pictures of Peter at his tennis best were off the wall and on the floor around him. He could barely remember doing that, but it wasn't the first time. Another weekend lost. Another weekend gone to shit.

He groaned and stood up, dizzy, and groped his way to the bedroom. A shower and a shave would fix him up just right. Hey, Peter was in England. Didn't that make up for a lot? Sure it did. Sure it did.

He showered, shaved, donned clean work clothes, remembered that there was a load of wash still in the washer that would have to be rewashed before it could be dried, grabbed his tool belt and left for work.

If Peter left for England on Sunday, maybe he'd hear from him by Friday. It wasn't much, but at least it was something to look forward to. The first thing, in fact, he'd had to look forward to since Fran's diagnosis.

JANUARY

Tess sipped her beer and slowly fingered the hair that was growing on her legs as they watched the conclusion of General Hospital. Peter sat straight up, engrossed in the drama. Tess was becoming involved, day by day, with the fictional characters and their dramatic lives, but she hadn't a real passion for it. Not like Peter.

She looked down at her crossed legs, then stretched them out in front of her. She'd never seen them so hairy. The hair was blonde, slightly red, and soft. It was nice. That had been her Christmas present to Peter. He wanted her to quit shaving under her arms and her legs, to quit using deodorant and makeup. She had agreed, and it was oddly pleasant. His Christmas present to her was a charming pledge of devotion and protection, delivered in poem form on Christmas morning. He also agreed to never run out of Heineken, and so the store down the block delivered two cases every week with the other groceries they ordered.

She watched the familiar pattern of freckles that were scattered across Peter's back as the General Hospital music came up, signaling the end of the show. He turned to her, leered, raised his eyebrows and said, "What now, my dear?"

She found the remote control under the blanket and clicked the television off.

Tess' heart turned over with affection for this man. "Cuddle," she said, and he took her in his arms. She felt his penis rise against her thigh, and she moved around to accommodate him. He slid inside and they lay together, entwined, thinking private thoughts. This is the best life could ever be, Tess thought, as she felt full with him. Peter loves me exactly the way I am.

She thought back to when she finally had the courage to show herself to him, naked, in her entirety, horrible scar on her belly and all. He had kissed her scar. He had kissed her scar! In that moment, she had been sealed to him for eternity. He liked the way she looked in the morning, he liked the way she smelled. All over. He liked her conversation, her humor, the way she made love, the way she played his games.

And he protected her. He saved her from the outside world, from outside problems and prejudices, from interference, from confrontations. He sheltered her, fed her, filled her body and spirit, and nourished her soul with ever-new ideas and concepts. She could be herself with Peter. She could be all those people she ever wanted to be: the baby, the little girl, the brat, the mother, the teacher, and he loved them all, he loved them all. She never wanted to leave. Except that Peter was all that, did all that, and she did nothing, really. Nothing except keep him company. She was afraid he would soon tire of her, and a little fear churned inside of her all the time.

"Tessa?"

"Peter?"

"Do you believe in God?"

"Um-hmm, I do. Do you?"

"I didn't, until I met you. Now I believe that there must be a God, because he answered my prayers. Tell me about your God."

She thought back to Sunday school, the few times she'd gone to church, with friends, with Charles's mother. She tried to think of something to say. "I don't know. I guess I've never thought much about Him. Merciful, I guess. Kind. I don't know. Listens to prayers. Answers them sometimes."

"Why do you suppose He listens when He doesn't answer them very often?"

"What do you mean?" Talk of religion always made Tess a little bit impatient.

"Well, I prayed about my hip, you know, to heal so I could play tennis."

"But if you played tennis, you and I would never have met."

Peter was silent.

"God has plans, I guess," Tess said.

"Think it's all predestination?"

"I don't know. Maybe."

He moved inside her. "Can you come?"

"I could."

"Want to?"

"Do you?"

He pulled out, leaving her feeling suddenly cold and

empty. "No. I want to go to the library. C'mon."

They both jumped out of bed and began their daily routine. Tess took the dishes to the kitchen and loaded the dishwasher while Peter stripped the bed and put the sheets in the washer. Then he jumped into the shower while she got fresh sheets out, and then jumped into the shower with him. He got out, dried off and made the bed with fresh, white sheets while she finished in the bathroom.

Only this time, when Tess came into the bedroom, toweling her hair, instead of seeing him freshly showered and in a fresh bed, beckoning her to join him, she saw him putting his jeans on.

She didn't want to go out, and she didn't want him to go out, either.

"Peter?"

"Hmm?"

She knelt by his feet. "Let's stay in."

"No, c'mon. I want to go to the library."

"Why?"

"God. I've got to find out about God."

"Watch TV on Sunday morning."

"No, no, Tessa, c'mon, let's go. Let's go get some books. We can read to each other."

"I don't want to go out." She sank to the floor and hugged his knees.

He stroked her hair. "Are you afraid?"

She nodded.

"The library is close. We'll hurry. Come on. Get dressed.

We can be back here in twenty minutes."

Tess looked at the clock. Twenty minutes was a long time. A lot could happen in twenty minutes. Peter could be hit by a bus, or see another woman, or they could lose each other in the crowd, or she could see Charles, or...her arms tightened their hold on Peter's legs.

"C'mon. I'll hold you."

She stood up, still shaky with the thought of being outside, in the world, with all those strangers, afraid of losing the man who had become her life, and she found her jeans and slipped them on. They bagged in the seat. She'd lost weight. She put a sweater on and tossed her hair. "Okay," she said. "Hold on to me and don't let me go."

He took her hand and they went out into the January morning.

The air was cold and smelly. It smelled like diesel exhaust. The air was thick with stench and noise.

"Oh, Peter, let's go back. Can't we call someone and order some books?"

"Come on, my Contessa," he said, and began to steer her down the street. But Tess felt him tense up as they entered the mainstream of foot traffic along the sidewalk.

Soon they were running. Arms entwined, hands in coat pockets, they shouldered their way through the crowd without regard to who they bumped shoved. They made a path like two trailblazers in the jungle. They didn't stop until they'd run up the steps to the library and through the big glass and wood doors into the dry heat and smell of books and old librarians.

He pulled her into the corner, next to the phone booth, and they held each other until they caught their breath. His fear was infectious and Tess found herself almost immobilized by it. "I hate this, Peter," she said, and he hugged her close.

They'd only been out of the apartment once since their trip to her place for clothes. That was for food at the corner deli, which, they discovered, would deliver. That had been six weeks ago. For six weeks, the apartment had been their entire universe. They controlled the heat, the television, the sheets, the food. They controlled their environment, their thoughts. The only intrusion was the telephone. Sometimes it rang for no reason, and they held each other on the bed and watched it until it stopped.

Tess sometimes thought about her apartment across town, cold and barren, alone, with no inhabitant for warmth. Sometimes she thought of her bank account, accumulating, she assumed, since she spent no money, except for rent and utilities on that empty space. She wondered, sometimes, how much money she had, how much money she would have, and then Peter would move or murmur or say something and that whole unreal world of money and lifeless apartments would disappear. It was unreal. Until now, standing in the library, it was all too real, and Tess was afraid of being out of control, afraid of outside influences, afraid of fates lurking... afraid.

"Let's go home," Peter said.

Tess's mouth was so dry she could barely speak. She

nodded against his chest, then heard him say, "Ready? Set? Let's go."

They pushed the heavy doors open again and gasped at the blast of frigid air. They ran down the library steps, holding tight to each other, and retraced their mad dash to the library as they ran back, aching to feel the comfort of home, longing to feast their frozen nostrils on the smell of their lair, skin itching to be free of clothes and back into clean, white sheets.

They pulled open the door of Peter's apartment building and ran through the lobby. Without waiting for the elevator they ran up the concrete fire stairs to the fourth floor. They burst out into the hall, still running, both of them out of breath. Peter unlocked the door, pulled Tess inside, shut the door, turned the deadbolt and they leaned against it.

They hugged, catching their breath, and Peter began to laugh. At first, Tess was puzzled, but she smiled, and then the relief tumbled out of her in giggles. She laughed with relief that nothing had happened to him, relief that she hadn't done, seen or heard anything damaging, relief that they were back inside, safe. It seemed like such a close call.

"Come on," Peter said, pulling her back toward the bedroom. "Hurry," he said, as they undressed. He jumped onto the bed, and before Tess had her shirt off, he pulled her over on top of him and thrust deeply inside. "Oh God, I just wanted to be inside you," he whispered. "Oh God, I was so afraid out there."

Tess listened as she rocked back and forth on him, feeling warm and delicious, comfortable and wanted. This was home.

This was life. This was heaven. What he was saying surprised her; she felt his fear, his anxiety, and it fueled hers which in turn refueled his. But to hear him say it was melodious.

She opened her eyes and looked down on him, his face drawn as he stared at her. "Afraid of what, Peter?"

He stopped moving. "Losing you. Losing you to the city," he said.

"You'll never lose me," she said, took a moment to savor the truth of that statement, then she bent down and kissed him deeply.

* * *

As dusk settled in from the outside, Peter spoke in a hushed tone. His voice startled Tess; they must have been silent for a long time.

"I still need to know about God," he said.

Tess looked up at him, leaning against the headboard with his hands behind his head. "I think you are God," she said.

His eyebrows went up. He was silent for a moment. "If I am, then so are you."

"Maybe we are."

"We are creative," he said.

"And apart—separated from the rest."

Peter sat up, clearly excited. "Then I can know all about God by studying you." He took her chin in his hand. "You and I are the universe." He slid down the bed, brought his pillow down, and reached for Tess. She loved the way he pulled her toward him. He always moved her around when they were making love—she loved the way he just took charge of her body and moved it where he wanted it. She let him slide her over closer to him, and she put one arm underneath him and they wrapped their legs around and he said, "Then we must have a purpose and a mission. Tell me. First, tell me everything about you."

"You mean my past?"

"Everything. Past, present, future, hopes, dreams, failures, fears, embarrassments, loves, likes, hates, everything. Everything."

Tess looked inside. There didn't seem to be much of a story to tell. "I don't have too much to say."

"Yes, you do," Peter said. "You've lived...how many years?"

"Thirty-four."

"Thirty-four years that I know nothing about. I want to know everything."

"But that might take a long time."

"We have eternity."

"I don't know where to start."

"It doesn't matter," Peter said. He kissed her forehead. "Just start."

Tess took a deep breath. "My mother was a nurse. She always smelled like Clorox, and she starched my clothes until they gave me rashes." Tess moved around in the bed, strangely uncomfortable inside her skin. Talking about her mother was something she'd always wanted to do, but she'd never had anyone to talk with before. Now that she had a chance, a safe chance—her mother was long dead and Peter was the perfect confidant—she was eager to purge her soul, but the words came out slowly, painfully. She felt like a new bottle of ketchup. She thought with a little prodding, the deluge might come, and that would be fine. That would be fine. She snuggled back up to Peter and began to prod herself. This was her chance to understand her mother, her chance to understand herself.

"She was a big woman, red-haired and freckled like me, but her hands were always rough and hard, and she was never gentle and loving with me. She dressed me in plain clothes when I was little, and when I grew old enough to have a taste of my own, she wouldn't let me buy my own things. I never bought my own clothes until I was married.

"She was never mean to me; I know she loved me. She was happy when I married Charles, he had such a brilliant future ahead of him, and she was proud to have molded a daughter that would be attractive to a man like that, and I guess that's part of the reason I married him, I wanted to please her so much. I spent my whole life trying to please her. But she was always so matter-of-fact. She was never spontaneous or fun, and I used to be afraid she would think me silly and frivolous all the time, but now that I think about it, I think she was envious of my good humor." This thought made Tess pause and rethink a few incidents. It was true, she discovered. Her mother had been envious. Peter twitched in impatience for her to continue.

"Life was not fun for Mama. A drifter, I guess, had gotten her pregnant when she was in her last year of nursing school, and she finished the year in shame. Sometime in there, I guess, she'd decided that life was hard, and so it was for her. She did her duty on this earth by raising me up, and right after I married Charles, she died."

Tess thought about the funeral, how she had made all the arrangements alone—Charles had been busy.

"What is it?"

"Oh, I was just thinking about Mama's funeral."

"Tell me."

"Well, it was surprisingly easy. I mean, I felt guilty for not feeling horrified or bereft or mournful or all of those things. But it was as if Mama and I were finished. She had mothered me, I guess I had daughtered her, and when I got married, it was over. All that was left was for her to die, and so she did. Strange."

Peter kissed her fingertip.

"Anyway, all her affairs were in order, and I inherited all her stuff. Most of it I sold, a few things are still in storage, I never brought them into the house I shared with Charles, and never had time to take them to the apartment. But Charles wouldn't even go to the funeral with me. Wouldn't you think that a man would be with his wife when her mother dies? And then when I had the miscarriage, Charles was too busy to see me in the hospital. And then the operation, you know, the one that...where they removed.... Anyway, Charles never came to visit, never sent flowers."

Peter kissed her palm.

"Maybe that's why Mama liked him. He was like her.

Determined, successful, but cold."

Peter pulled her to him and rubbed his hands around her back.

"And you never knew about your father?"

"Nothing. Mama started me on the pill when I was sixteen, even though Charles was the first man I slept with, and I never slept with him until I was nineteen. She just told me that women are prone to moments of weakness, and it's just as well to avoid mistakes. As far as I know, Mama only slept with a man once in her life, and that resulted in me."

"Poor Mama."

Tess giggled and gave Peter a kiss on the shoulder. "Poor Mama," she echoed. "For a while I thought about staging a nationwide campaign to find him. Place full page ads in all the newspapers, you know, 'Whoever slept with a red-headed nurse one September in Chicago, please call this number to meet your adult daughter.' Can you imagine?" Tess remembered her short but fiercely intense obsession with finding him. "But then it really doesn't matter. He was nothing but a sperm in the right place at the right time." She kissed Peter again. "Hey, when are we going to talk about you?"

"Later. I'm still interested in your father."

"Well I've got nothing more to say." She knew this wasn't true. The resentments and old anger—the fury—still lay like plastic shrinkwrap around her childhood. She was never worthy of having a father. Of two parents. Of being loved. Maybe he knew about her all along but he didn't want her.

Maybe her mother had lied to her all those years; maybe Tess's father knew her and didn't like her. All those old thoughts and questions still churned, still burned, and she ached to let them out. But this wasn't the time. Maybe there would never be a time.

"I think you do have more to say."

"I hated him for a time. I was always mad at him—I guess I still am."

"What else?"

"Nothing else. He's not a part of my life."

"You never think about him?"

"Sure I do. I wonder what he'd think of me today, I wonder if I'd recognize him on the street, I wonder if I look like him at all. Sometimes I stop whatever I'm doing and wonder if he'd approve of who I am and how I look and what I do." She felt tears, but resisted them.

"You want him to be proud of you."

"Of course. Don't you want your parents to be proud of you?"

Peter parried the question. "Tell me about not being able to have children."

Tess's insides seized up. She never wanted to talk about this, not to anybody. She forced her muscles to relax, one by one. "I'm tired, Peter," she said. "Can we talk later?"

His big hands caressed her back. "Sure," he said, and she snuggled into his chest.

* * *

When they awoke, Peter took two minutes to run to the

bathroom and then the kitchen, and was back with a cherry pie and two forks.

The clock said ten-thirty p.m.

They ate the pie and then sat back, stuffed.

"I still need to know, Tessa."

Tess tensed. "Know what, Peter?" But she knew what he meant.

"How it is for you, not to be able to get pregnant, to have kids."

"Why do you need to know that stuff?"

Peter turned to her, wrapped one leg around hers, took her face in his hands. She loved it when he touched her face with his big hands. "Because I just love you so much," he said. "I just love you so much I could never have believed it before I met you that I could ever love someone this much. I've got to know everything about you, inside and out, because that's what makes love stronger."

"But it takes time to know things about people."

"We don't have time, Tessa. We only have now, right now, remember?"

"Eternity, remember?"

"But what is eternity, if it isn't the eternal now?"

He has an answer for everything, she thought. She slumped.

He nuzzled her, then brought her face up. She looked into the sparkle of those blue eyes. "Please, Tessa. I agree, if we were dating every Saturday night and planned to be married and live in the suburbs, that it would take a long time to know each other. But we've chosen a different way. We are special, and our togetherness is special. We can't expect anything about us to be average. So tell me. Let me know you."

"I had a tubal pregnancy," Tess started out slowly. "And they had to remove the tube. They told me not to get pregnant for six months while everything healed, and then after that, I couldn't get pregnant. We tried everything. Charles was more frustrated than I was, if that's possible, and then the only thing left was for them to go in and look around. They found my other tube was completely blocked, deformed, actually, I guess, and so they took it out and my uterus, too. And that was that.

"I knew right away that things had changed with Charles after that. Having an heir was so important to him. I don't think we ever made love again after that. He waited around until I healed, until I got back on my feet, and then he began to tell me, slowly, in little hints, that I should be preparing myself for going out on my own." She felt Peter draw back from her a little bit, and she wanted to stop talking, but it was too late. She kept going.

"At first, I tried to tell myself that it was okay, that physical problems occur. And so do marital problems. One had nothing to do with the other. It wasn't my fault, after all, it was just one of those things. And then I knew the truth. Charles made me face the truth. He didn't want me any more if I couldn't give him what he thought was his right as a male. And then I realized that I was an inferior member of the species, because it's only the fittest that reproduce, and I was not able to perpetuate my line." Tears began to choke her. Familiar tears. "I used to see pregnant women parading their big bellies around town and I'd die inside. I'd see a man carrying a baby and I'd just lose it. I'd cry for hours. My entire body was made for one purpose only, and that's to bear and rear children, and I couldn't. I couldn't." She hiccupped and then blew her nose on a tissue that Peter offered. "My father never carried me and Charles would never carry our children. You have no idea what it's like. I'm not a woman, I'm a shell of a woman. I'm an empty box that looks like a woman, at least that's what Charles finally said, when he asked for his divorce. Then he moved all my things into that apartment and that was the end of it." She sniffled, wiped her nose and swelling eyes, and looked up at Peter, who stared at her without expression.

"Please don't look at me like that," she said. "I'm afraid that you'll throw me out, too."

"Tessa, Tessa, Tessa," Peter said. "You are the most wonderful, most desirable, sexiest, most complete woman in the world. I have never met a woman who pleased me as much as you have."

Tess sniffed. "Sure," she said.

"I mean it. See?"

And she saw that she had indeed aroused him, and wondered briefly if it was her misery that was attractive, and then they were making love, and she felt full, and not like a shell at all.

When she awoke later that night, Peter was sleeping, all curled up on his side, with both hands tucked under his pillow. He looked like a child, like a baby, and Tess realized that having this man in her life was better than having any baby for Charles. Peter saw through her hurt and torment, and helped heal it. Charles only picked at her scabs until they became scars. Peter wanted the whole of them exposed to the universe for acceptance, while Charles hid most of his life in his filing cabinet.

She leaned over and kissed Peter's temple, and in his sleep, he reached out, drew her near, and as his mouth found her breast and he gently sucked her nipple, she knew that the mysterious God had answered her prayers as well.

* * *

In the morning, when Peter punched the "on" button on the television remote control, he heard the familiar whine of power, but nothing happened on the screen. He punched the button on and off several times, then climbed over Tess, who was sleeping crossways on the bed, and slammed the side of the TV with his hand. Nothing. No picture, no sound. He climbed back, tried the bedside light. It worked. He looked up at the digital clock on top of the television. It read 7:55. He flipped channels, fiddled with all the dials, but nothing.

"Shit."

"What is it?" Tess's sleepy voice came up from under a wad of sheet.

"Television's broke," he said, and he felt like crying.

"Oh, no."

"Yeah. Well." He took a grip on his emotions and squeezed. What began as a whine (Nothing's ever right for me, nothing ever turns out okay. Why me, what the fuck have I done?) was clenched into a hot rod of anger. (Who needs it anyway? It's just a dumb box.) He got out of bed, unplugged the television, unplugged the clock, picked them both up and staggered through the bedroom, through the kitchen, to the front door. God, they were heavy. Heavier than he'd ever imagined. His heart pounded, and his face filled with blood by the time he leaned them up against the wall, propped up with one knee, by the apartment door. He opened it, looked both ways down the hall. The coast was clear. Who needs this trash?. Not me. I don't need this shit cluttering up my life. With a gasp, he heaved, and the two appliances tumbled down the hall, dragging their cords behind them. Peter stood in the hallway, hands on hips, feet apart, naked and bearded, and he laughed. Then he sauntered back inside the apartment, slammed the door and went back to bed, hoping Tess had seen him.

She looked at him with amazement in her eyes. He liked that. He touched her chin, then got up again, took the calendar from the kitchen cabinet, the little alarm clock in the living room, picked up his cell phone, opened the door and threw them out, too.

But the man across the hall opened his door just before Peter got his closed. Peter saw that the man saw him and fear shot through him.

"Hey," the guy said, but Peter slammed the door, locked

it, ran back into the bedroom and hugged Tess.

Soon there was knocking on the door, and voices outside, and more knocking, and then pounding. Peter held onto Tess, and they watched the bedroom door, and listened.

Shortly thereafter, Peter heard the building manager's voice. "You can't just throw your trash into the hall. Come out and pick these things up. Come on, now. Come on, before I call the cops." Peter felt his chest relaxing, as he realized that his rent was paid, the deadbolt had been thrown, nobody could or would come in. Someone would want those time things, anyway. Nobody would grumble too loudly.

Soon the pounding and the shouts and the muttering stopped, and Peter began to smile. "No television," he said. "No clocks, no calendars, no time. From now on, we practice eternity. Our togetherness happens outside of time. We can live an entire lifetime in a moment, or cause our orgasms to last for years. We can do anything we want, can't we, my goddess, my Contessa?"

Tess's blue eyes looked at him with wonder, and he felt the power that she'd given him surge through his body. He laughed aloud, then stood on the bed, feet spread, arms out as if to embrace the atmosphere, and he laughed again. "I am King Peter," he said, and saw his lovely lady giggling into her hand. "And you, fair maiden, are Queen Tessa." He held out his hand and she took it, then with a royal gesture, he lifted her to her feet, and she joined him, standing on the bed, standing by his side, King and Queen of all of creation as they knew it.

Fran would have loved this, Peter thought, as they sat down, then lay back on the bed, his arm wrapped around a silent Tess. Fran would completely approve of the king and queen and their eternal now. Arnie was always saying, "If I were King," and Peter would look at his mother and they would laugh with him, but they also laughed at him a bit, because he had never been a king and would never be a king and everybody knew it.

And if Arnie wanted to be king, well then Peter wanted to be God.

And he would be. He was.

Thinking about Fran made Peter smile; thinking about Arnie made his chest feel tight. He kissed Tess on the side of her head and thought about all the approving things Fran would say about her.

*   *   *

It took probably three weeks for the realization to dawn on Arnie that Peter wasn't in England at all. His suspicion began when a week went by without a call or a text, but he rationalized it away. Then two weeks went by and he began to worry, especially since he didn't know who Peter was meeting with. And slowly the realization dawned. He even realized that when Peter told him he was going to England, Arnie hadn't believed it. He hadn't even believed him then, but he wanted to. He wanted to believe so badly. He wanted Peter to do something with himself, something—anything—as long as it was important to Peter.

Apparently, shutting his father out of his life was

important to Peter. He'd be gone a couple of days to a month, he'd said. Why? He's sick. He's shacking up. He's cooking something up. The truth of it stung Arnie far deeper than anything else ever had. For three weeks he'd not fallen into a fit of depression. Every time the loneliness threatened to overcome him, he thought of his successful, good looking young son out there in England, making deals to be an announcer, a promoter, something on the pro tennis circuit. He could live through his son if he had no other life to live.

And so he had gone about his business as an electrician, wiring, rewiring, finding problems, all the time thinking about what Peter was thinking today, doing today, who he was talking to. The days rushed by with a nice smoothness, the kind of smoothness Arnie hadn't felt since, well, since before Fran died, since before Peter's accident. When they were a family.

Peter's life meant everything to Arnie, and now he had been deliberately, maliciously shut out of it.

It hurt. God, it hurt.

His boots were so heavy he could hardly walk. On Friday, he told his partner he didn't feel well and went home early, picked up a bottle of Jack Daniel's on the way, and headed straight for a long weekend.

FEBRUARY

"I don't want to hear any more about Charles," Peter said.

Tess looked at him in amazement. "You wanted to hear all about my life," she said.

"I know, but I'm tired of hearing his name." Peter picked at his toes.

"He was such a big part of—"

"I know. I know, I know, I know. But he's not anymore, and I can't stand the thought of his hands on you. How he screwed those women, washed off his prick and then came home and stuck it into you. I want us to forget that time. I want all of our energies to be put into the now, into the today, into just us."

"My past is a part of me," Tess said, feeling off balance. She was mystified. Again. Every time she thought she understood, Peter put her off balance. Again.

"I know, my darling, but let's just acknowledge that entire glob of history has somehow molded you into the wonderful person you are today, and let's not talk about it anymore."

"But all we've done is talk about me. I haven't heard about you."

"There's nothing worth knowing, really."

Tess pouted. "Not fair," she said.

"Okay. Encapsulated. I grew up in a middle-class Chicago suburb. My parents were normal, hard-working people. I am an only child. Mother died last year from liver cancer. I miss her. My dad's an electrician for a big construction outfit. He coached me and saw me through all the junior tennis championships. When I turned pro, he was thrilled. I was just starting to make a name for myself when a drunk driver careened through my life and destroyed my career. I've been nothing since. Until that night when I met you at Mario's. And since then, I've been everything I've always wanted to be. My life has been heaven." He leaned over and kissed her.

Tess smiled.

"And that's that."

Tess stood up and looked out the window. The city was filthy. Sooty snow mixed with salt crystals lay everywhere, looking ugly. She turned and looked at Peter on the bed. Peter, blonde, white-skinned with his reddish beard, lay stretched out on tousled white sheets. She remembered seeing a movie where they photographed people sleeping together on a bed, and speeded up the film. The camera was located in the ceiling, looking directly down upon the bed. The people tossed and turned, wrapping up in covers, throwing covers off, cuddling, separating, cuddling again, and Tess thought at the time that it was like looking through a microscope at a slide of two organisms in the throes of their life.

She wondered what it would look like to an audience if

there were a camera in the ceiling of this room. She and Peter lived their life on the microscopic slide of his white-sheeted bed, both of them losing weight, losing muscle tone—they'd been in bed together for over two months. They ate in bed, they slept in bed, they talked in bed, they made love in bed. They did everything except shower and go to the toilet in this bed.

And now Peter was alone in the bed and she was looking at him from the ceiling point of view, and he looked small and terribly alone. She pulled the curtains closed and joined him.

"Okay, Peter," she said. "If we don't talk about the past, and we don't talk about the future, what do we talk about?"

Peter was silent. He turned over on his side, away from her. Tess had come to know this gesture, it was Peter's way of having some time to himself, of being alone, of wanting to be left alone. She respected his wishes, turned on her side, her back to him, and she thought about her life: past, present and future.

The past had been nothing but heartache, it was true. Charles was a cold man. There had never been warmth and love in their marriage, at least not in the ways that Hollywood always showed. There was never even passion. Charles had a methodical approach to lovemaking, and it was never spontaneous or exciting. But Charles made it clear to her that he was the best Tess could ever hope for, so she put up with his cool life and his expensive mistresses and got on with life, the rock of disappointment adding weight to her marriage.

And then when the time came for Charles to be rid of her, she felt cast adrift. She talked to "friends"—acquaintances, really. In Charles's social circle, nobody had real friends. She realized that she would have to go through the husband-hunting scene because she had no skills, no way to support herself. No desire to support herself. And she was so afraid of being out there, of dating, of having to do all those things that single people did as they approached middle age with scars on their belly and scars on their psyche. It had been nightmare stuff. Nightmare stuff.

Peter didn't want to talk about the past, and that was wise. The past was nothing but disappointment. And the future was made of fear. Peter was wise to not want to talk about the future, either, because they could only speculate, and everything possible in life that did not include being on this bed, together with him, was horrible to think about.

Tess always worked double time, over time, to try to make Charles take notice of her. The relationship—even though Peter didn't want to use that word, that's what it was—with Peter was hot and heavy. He did nothing else but take notice of her. The two extremes in her life.

Living with Peter was more like an experiment. And that's appropriate, she thought, for two people who live on a microscopic slide.

She turned over onto her back and looked at the back of his neck. His breathing was regular and deep, it looked as though he'd fallen asleep. There won't be another for man me, she realized. This one is it. I will give this relationship my best shot, one hundred percent, my total energy, and if it doesn't work out—a horrible taste came to her mouth—then I won't even try again. I won't even try.

Okay, Peter, she thought. No past, no future.

Bye-bye, Mama. She remembered that some of her mother's things and some of her grandmother's things were still in storage. Nobody was paying the rent on them. They'd be auctioned off if she didn't. She didn't need them. Peter didn't want her to have them. It wasn't important. Those things weren't important. She'd lived without them. She wouldn't even miss them.

Bye, Charles. I hope you find happiness, even though I know you never will. Well, maybe a son will make you happy.

Bye-bye, Carolyn. Standing me up at Mario's that night was perhaps the best thing, perhaps the worst thing, you ever did for me. You were the closest thing I ever had to a friend.

Bye-bye, dreams of becoming a dancer, of becoming the doting mother of a teenager. No more thoughts of babysitting for the grandchildren, of having everybody over for a twenty-pound turkey on a frosty Thanksgiving day. No more thoughts of writing the memoirs of being involved with Charles and his strange society life, no more thoughts of being on The Tonight Show, no more thoughts of even watching The Tonight Show again, probably.

Bye-bye, bulging belly with life inside. That option had disappeared a long time ago, but maybe this time she could really choose to not have children instead of leaving that choice up to fate or whatever. I would rather have Peter, I really would, she thought.

Even so, a tear slipped out, her breath ragged in her chest.

She reached over and opened the nightstand drawer. There was a tissue and a sixpack of Heineken. She blew her nose, ever so quietly, so as to not waken Peter, and she opened a warm beer.

She swigged, burped quietly, drank more. She looked down at her legs, then slipped them out from under the sheet. They were thin, yet well formed, but they were not dancer's legs. All those things that were in her past and all those dreams for the future had been decided for her. Her reluctance to let go of those things was silly. Peter was right. All we have is the here and now. Here. On this slide. In this bed. Next to this sleeping man. And now. Drinking a beer, softly weeping for no good reason.

Here and now. Of course. Here and now. The experience of a lifetime, all right here, right now. On this bed.

"Open one for me, too, Tessa," Peter said, his voice startling her in the quiet of the bedroom.

"I thought you were sleeping."

"I was thinking." He rolled over and stroked her arm. She set her beer on the nightstand while she opened him a fresh one.

"Me, too."

"You're sad."

"Not really. Just kind of cleaning out the mental filing cabinet, I guess. Throwing out ancient history. Some of it hurts a little."

"I know," Peter said, and took a pull on his beer. "This is it for me, you know."

"It?"

"Yeah. It." He put his arm under her and brought her close to him, but kept staring at the ceiling. He was silent for a moment, taking little sips from his beer. "You and me. You are so perfect—" Tess began to squirm. "Settle down, now," Peter said, "I'm trying to say something. Just listen, and accept me, okay?" Tess snuggled down into his side. "You are so perfect for me, you are so perfect yourself. And the way that you love me, the way that you are willing to do just about anything we think is good—well, I just can't imagine having anyone else in my life. If, for some reason, you and I don't work out, then I'll be celibate and a recluse."

Tess felt the truth of this shudder through his body. "Me, too," she said.

"Really?"

"Really. I was just thinking that same thing."

"That's great! That means we're even more on a wavelength than I thought."

"But Peter..."

"Yes, my darling?"

"What's it for? I mean what's it about?"

"We are God, remember?"

Tess nodded.

"The yin and the yang," he said. "One cannot be without the other. The black and the white. The good and the bad. We are the whole. Apart, we are nothing, we have been nothing, we would be nothing. Together we are everything. The duality."

"But who are we helping? Isn't the purpose of life to help others?"

"Aren't we helping each other?"

"I guess so." Sometimes the things Peter said confounded Tess. She tried to keep up, tried to coordinate his ideas with those she'd lived with for thirty-four years. It was a stretch.

"Well, maybe we need to help each other first. I don't feel totally healed yet, yet I'm so much stronger, so much better than I was when we first met. It's only been two months, Tess. Let's give it time."

Tess looked at how uncomfortable she had been throughout her entire life, and how that discomfort had faded away during these past two months. She was totally and completely at ease with Peter—he accepted her. She, too, was healing, she realized. And yet she was not wholly well. It would take time, Peter was right. "Peter?"

"Hmm?"

"Will you marry me?"

"Yes, of course. Absolutely. Right now? The merging of the dualities. Of course. Let's do it right now."

"No, let's think about it and do it right."

"Okay," he said, and drained his beer. Then he sat up straight. "What are your thoughts?"

"Well, I think we should write our vows."

"Right."

"And have a little ceremony."

"Okay."

"That's all."

"I'll get paper." Peter jumped out of bed, ran into the kitchen and returned with a roll of paper towels and two pens. "You write your vows and your ceremony and I'll write mine and then we'll do it."

Tess, caught up again in the magic of the madness of this man and his twinkling eyes, grabbed a pen, tore off three towels and began to write.

They worked for three days. They wrote, crossed out, erased, tore the paper, rewrote, and wrote some more. Tess tried to reach down inside her soul for the words that conveyed the meaning of her feelings, and she found words sadly lacking. She continued to write, her promises and vows becoming ever longer, ever more complex as she endeavored to explain herself to her man.

She diligently resisted the temptation to sneak peeks at what Peter wrote, even though he blatantly tried to look at her papers. There were times of terrible curiosity, though, especially when he was sleeping, his papers scattered about him, but she never looked. She never looked. She wasn't so sure about him, she thought he read her stuff while she slept, but it didn't matter, it was all love and fun and commitment. And she was a bride-to-be, and that was the best part.

A bride to be and she hadn't had to date.

For three days she sweat and worked, knowing all the time that she'd never get it quite right, she'd never really be able to express to Peter what she felt, yet she tried, she tried.

Each time she felt finished, she hoped against hope that it was complete, but each time she knew it wasn't. The merging of the dualities of God was a big ceremony.

And on the third day, Peter said, "Let's do it tomorrow morning." Tess smiled at him, tentatively, knowing his vow to her would be ever so much bigger, better, greater, deeper, more wonderful than hers to him, and the anticipation was eating her alive.

She spent the third day copying the nine pages of vows, making additions, deletions and corrections, none of it sounding like Tess, none of it sounding good enough. And when bedtime came, she tossed and turned, unable to sleep, feeling that this was the first real test of Peter-and-Tess, and she was about to fail.

How on earth could she pledge her soul to this man when she didn't even know her own self?

And then, in that quiet period just before dawn, when the world slept and Peter snored quietly by her side, she knew the answer. She knew the perfect vow, and it didn't include nine pages of nonsense and abstract commotion. She knew within herself the extent of this vow, and it was simple and it was everything.

She slept.

In the morning, he awakened her with a kiss on the neck. "Contessa, my bride."

She awoke with a start, and looked at Peter, and they both laughed, then jumped out of bed, Tess ran to the shower, while Peter grabbed up all the dishes from around the bed.

He threw them into the dishwasher and then jumped into the shower just as Tess was finishing. She stripped the bed, throwing the soiled sheets into the washing machine and then she remade the bed with clean, white sheets. Anticipation jittered in her belly.

She got a cold sixpack of Heineken from the refrigerator and a package of sticky assorted Danish, grabbed up some napkins and was waiting for him when he walked, toweling off, back into the bedroom.

Peter carefully combed his hair, then sat on the edge of the bed. "Ready?"

Tess nodded, feeling light and flushed.

"You first?"

Tess nodded again, then swallowed hard. "Okay," she said. "Come sit here, facing me." They sat cross-legged on the bed. Tess touched Peter's face with both of her hands. She looked right into his eyes. She wanted to remember this moment.

"Where're your papers?"

"Shhh." She touched his face with her fingertips, his eyes, his nose, his lips, cheeks, chin, and then ran them down his neck, over his shoulders, across his chest to his belly, down over his thighs and down his calves, then up again to his shoulders and down his arms to his fingertips. She held his fingers lightly in her own. "King Peter, I wish to live with you here in Candyland forever."

She waited for his response. He was clearly waiting for more. After all, she'd written and rewritten all those pages.

She saw the dawning come over his face as he realized that was the end of it, and for a moment she felt like diving through a hole. It wasn't enough, it wasn't enough, I should have given it the whole shot, it wasn't good enough. She couldn't look at him and started to take her hands away in shame.

And then Peter started to laugh.

"That was great! Oh my God, that was incredible! My turn. My turn. Look at me."

She looked up and saw admiration in his face, and his hands came up to her cheeks, and he felt her face with his fingertips just as she'd felt his, and she felt his hands all over her just as his blue eyes looked directly into her innermost being, and when he finally took her hands in his, he said, "Queen Tessa, I wish to live with you here in Candyland forever."

And tears came to her eyes and tears came to his eyes and they hugged and kissed and then made the sweetest, most tender love ever, two newlyweds on clean, white sheets.

* * *

Peter lay awake as his bride slept the sleep of the sexually sated, and there was only one thing on his mind. Candyland.

What a concept.

Their life was a candyland, there was no doubt about that. They had as much sex, food and beer as they wanted. They had solitude and privacy. Security. Together they had enough money to do anything they wanted. But the key word here was "together." Life had been nothing but shitty before Tess came. She was just absolutely perfect. And her wedding ceremony. Jesus, he thought, it was so simple, so complete, so perfect.

Candyland. He felt so high, he thought winning Wimbledon could only be a flash in comparison. This would be lasting, and lasting.

We should be writing this down.

His heart began to pound. We should be writing this down. There's something here that is so extraordinary that other people could learn from our experience. Maybe we could sit here in the privacy of our own Candyland, and write a book about the experience. About the experiment. Maybe two people have never lived together the way we do. We're extraordinary. Surely people would want to hear about it. That's the purpose! Tessa wanted to know who we were helping. Nobody, yet, we had to experience it all first, but now we're ready. Now we're really ready.

He snuggled down to Tess and kissed her awake. "Princess? I've got an idea."

Tess cracked a puffy eye, smiled at him, then took a long, catlike stretch. Her little pink nipple shrunk down in the cold and he touched it. Tess laughed and pulled the sheet up over herself. "What?"

"What what?"

"What's your idea?"

"Oh, yeah." He looked at her freckled face, at her red curls in disarray, and for a moment, he was afraid. He was afraid that she would laugh at him, he was afraid that Candyland was not real, he was afraid he was losing his mind, he was afraid that if they did write it and sent it away, that people would want to see them, would want to talk to them, would make offers to them, and bust open their cocoon. Then their whole world would come crashing down around them and they would lose all they had. No, he thought, it's a bad idea. He knew he wouldn't succumb, but he didn't know how much he could trust Tess. He couldn't chance it. He needed to keep it the same. It can't change. I won't let it change. "Never mind."

"Never mind? You woke me up for a 'never mind'?"

"I just wanted to watch you wake up," Peter said, and touched the tip of her nose, but in the back of his mind, he wondered how much she really liked being here with him. He wondered if she was telling him the truth, the whole truth, all the time.

* * *

Arnie lounged in the chair facing his boss's desk with a fresh cup of steaming coffee. He'd been summoned, he assumed, because of the accident. His partner had fallen off a ladder, and there were always safety interviews and procedures.

Lee Adams came into the office and closed the door behind him. "We think you ought to think about taking some time off, Arnie," he said as he plopped himself down into his loose, squeaky desk chair.

"Time off?" This hit Arnie right out of left field.

"A couple of weeks."

"A couple of weeks?" His mind reeled. "I...I don't

understand."

Lee sighed, then hauled himself back up out of that chair. He walked around the edge of his desk then sat with one cheek on the corner of it. Arnie had the feeling he'd seen this scene in too many movies. "You need a rest, Arnie. Your work is getting sloppy, you're making mistakes. Al could have been hurt yesterday, you know, hurt bad. You set that ladder, and it wasn't right. The other guys have been covering for you, and they were happy to do it for a while, but now you're sniping at them and being pretty ill-tempered and they're tired of it."

Arnie felt as if someone had thrown a bucket of boiling water in his face.

"So what do I do?" Lee went on. "You're a valuable guy. You've been with us a long time. We all like you. You've also been through a lot this year. So I want you to take a couple of weeks off. Get some rest. Take a trip. Do something to take the edge off."

"Listen, Lee. It's my boy."

Lee held his hand up, shook his head. "I know, Arnie. I know."

"No, you don't."

"Two weeks, Arnie. It's either that or I let you go."

Arnie slumped. "Okay. Two weeks."

"Our health plan covers therapy, you know."

"Don't need no goddamn shrink, Lee. I need my boy, and I don't know where he is."

"Well, you've got two weeks. Find him and spend some time with him. Two weeks, Arnie. Use it."

Arnie stood up. He couldn't meet Lee's eyes. He'd let his partners down, he'd let the company down, he'd let Lee down. He couldn't shake hands with him. He felt like putting his tail between his legs. He hadn't felt like this since he was sent to the principal's office in high school.

"Come back better, Arnie."

Arnie nodded and went out into the break room. All the guys were in there. They silenced when he came into the room. He held up his hand to his partner, Al, but he couldn't meet his eyes. He got his jacket from his locker and left.

He sat in his car, hands on the steering wheel. Suddenly he remembered being in bed with Fran one night. She was reading, her half-glasses so cute on her nose, her hair shining from having been brushed, and flowing around her shoulders, the way he liked it, the way she never wore it, except to bed. He remembered looking at her, knowing their young son was safely in the other room, their savings accounts were fairly fat, they didn't have many outstanding bills, life was good. Life was too good. Life was so good he didn't dare touch his beautiful wife for fear that it was all an illusion. He was afraid that if he touched her, that it would all turn bad, it would all have been a weird trick on him from the very beginning.

Had it been?

He started the car and pulled out of the lot. Two weeks was a lot of time to fill. That was one hell of an extended weekend. He didn't want to lose himself in it all for two fucking weeks.

He turned left, but he didn't want to go home. The house

was filled with that syrupy damned loneliness. If he went there, he would be awash. He could drown in two weeks. No, he would use the time. He would track down Peter and he would find out just exactly what the hell.

MARCH

"Just leave it," Tess said through the door. She heard the delivery boy put the boxes of food down, and she waited naked and shivering, until she was sure the elevator had come to get him. Then she opened the door a crack, looked at the two boxes, then looked both ways along the hall. No one in sight. She pulled the groceries inside and then shut the door, locked it, bolted it and slid the chain into place.

Resting on the top was an envelope. Tess opened it. It was a copy of the bill the grocery store would send to Peter's business manager. The total for the food came to thirty-seven dollars and twenty-nine cents, but what caught her eye was at the top. The date. March twenty-third.

March twenty-third.

She had been out of this apartment twice in the past four months, and not at all in over two months. That didn't seem possible. She looked into the living room and it looked cold, uninhabited. The kitchen floor hadn't been mopped or swept in all that time—they minimized the time they were out of bed, so no housework at all had been done. The toilet, in fact, was filthy, something Tess just hoped somebody else would take care of, like the maid always did at home.

March twenty-third. Time strode relentlessly on. She wondered for a moment why she should be astonished at this; time always kept going by, no matter what. Somehow, though, she felt as if time in this apartment was outside of that time slipstream that carried everyone else along. Her birthday approached. She would soon be thirty-five, and that too, sounded like an unreal fact. She didn't feel any older than she did when she was about twenty. She picked up a bag of marshmallows with her toes and listened to Peter in the shower. She was supposed to be making the bed up with clean sheets, and she should be putting the food away. Instead, she just thought about that date. March twenty-third.

She opened the marshmallows and popped one into her mouth, chewing slowly. March. In like a lion and out like a lamb. Spring. New buds on the trees, melting snow, rain, young love. She looked into the living room again. Yep. The fern was dead. She ate another marshmallow, then began to look in the boxes for the graham crackers and the chocolate. She found them, set them aside. Then she put the beer in the fridge, the ice cream in the freezer and left the rest on the kitchen floor. She took the s'mores makings into the bedroom along with two cold beers, made the bed and waited for Peter.

He came in, toweling off, and stepped up onto the bed. "Hey," he said. "What a beautiful day! Clean sheets, s'mores, a beautiful wife, what more could a man want?" He jumped up and down a couple of times and then sat down, took a graham cracker, half of Tess's Nestle's Crunch, a couple of marshmallows and began to try to put together a sandwich.

"Peter?"

"Hmmm?"

"What are we doing here?"

"Making a statement."

She'd never thought of that before. "What's our statement?"

"That life can be giggles and crunch." He crunched his graham cracker.

"Giggles and crunch?"

"Niggles and Grunch."

"Squiggles and Munch."

"Nirgles and Squnch."

Tess began to laugh. That's a good statement, she thought. So much of what used to be on television was worthless, depressing, bad news. Here, in the apartment, there was no bad news.

"But who to? Who's getting the statement?"

"God."

Tess fixed herself a marshmallow and chocolate sandwich on graham crackers and wished she'd brought in the peanut butter. It broke into pieces before she could eat it all, and she dusted herself and the bed off, then washed it all down with her Heineken. God. A statement to God.

"Hey, God," she said, as she held up her beer to him. "Smiggles and slunch."

Peter laughed and spit crackers all over the pillows. That was the funniest thing Tess had ever seen and she started to laugh and soon tears were running down their cheeks, and they had to hold on to each other to keep from falling off the bed, absolutely weak and helpless in their mirth.

Tess wiped the tears from her eyes, briefly wondering if she'd been crying in the middle of all that laughing, and looked at Peter, who was trying to calmly eat that impossible sandwich and she said, "Peter, you're the best."

"You are," he said, chewing.

"This is," she said, and he nodded in agreement.

"We need peanut butter to cement these damned things together," Peter said.

"Just what I was thinking," Tess said. She got up and went to the kitchen.

And there, on top of the groceries, was that invoice. March twenty-third. Soon she'd be thirty-five and then in another flash of time she'd be thirty-six, and then forty. Would she still be in this apartment? She picked up the invoice, and crumpled it in her hand, then threw it into the box of trash in the corner. Peter was right to throw out all the calendars, she thought. They were just the past and the future and all that is hurt and bitterness and pain and suffering. All that really matters is now. Now. Time and months and years and ages mean nothing. Nothing at all.

She took the peanut butter and two fresh beers back to bed.

"You okay?"

She nodded, sitting on the edge of the bed.

"What is it?"

What is it? she asked herself. It was loneliness, it was

restlessness. It was also gratitude for having the best of everything, yet there was so much else. Why must one give up the best in order to have more variety? It's time passing and passing. It's divorced and sterile. It's this trashy apartment and this magic bedroom. It's Peter and then again, it's Peter. What do I say to him? She kicked the mattress, brought her feet up underneath her and folded her arms. She bowed her head and looked at her hair as it fell around her face. What is it, anyway?

"Time," she finally said.

"I know."

It took a moment before she realized what he had said. He knew. Did he? Did he really?

She turned and looked at him, and she saw herself mirrored in his eyes. She saw that same wistfulness, of having it all and yet wanting more.

He held out his arms and she melted into them, the tears coming hard and fast. She clung to him while the sobbing took its course, shaking her body and his, their bed, their realm. Charles never held me when I cried, she thought, and that made her cry harder for all the time she had wasted.

When the storm was over, she felt tears other than her own, and she knew Peter had cried with her and that made it all worthwhile. Peter had cried with her. Peter had cried, and she had cried and maybe now they could get on with it.

On with what? Isn't that what made the tears come in the first place?

"Peter?"

"Hmmm?" He smoothed her hair and rubbed his big hands along her sides.

"We communicate—"

"—without talking."

She nodded against him. "More," she said.

"We should work on talking with hardly any words at all."

She nodded against him. "Further."

"No words."

She nodded. "Document."

He pushed her away, and she looked into his face. Fear had set in while she wasn't looking, and she looked deeper into his face, and deeper yet.

He was afraid of the documentation. He was afraid, not of the experiment, but of the results.

She sat up and ran her fingers over his face. She relaxed his worried look and kissed his cheek.

He understood. He needn't be afraid. They would do nothing without each other's approval. "Later," she whispered. He nodded, reached for her and held her close to him.

And then a knock came at the door.

Peter stiffened, and little beads of perspiration appeared as if by magic, all across his forehead.

"Peter? It's your father."

He tightened his grip on Tess's arm so hard it hurt her.

"Ow," she said, and he released her, but he paid no attention. He was listening to his father, who had started banging on the door.

"Peter! Open the door!"

Peter's knees drew up as he turned over on his side. Tess wrapped her arms tight around him, brought the sheet and blanket up over both of them. Graham cracker crumbs flew everywhere. She could hear his heart pounding.

"Peter! I know you're in there, son. Listen, I can help you. I know you have problems, but there's help. There's professional help. It won't be easy, boy, but we can see it through together, okay?" There was a long pause. "Peter, goddammit, don't make me call the manager. I'll break this fucking door down if you don't open it. I've been to Noble's office and they told me that they pay your bills. Food bills, Peter, every month. Food is delivered here every (bang) fucking (bang) week (bang)."

With every slam of his father's fist on the door, Peter's muscles jerked. Tess still held him, but he had gone from her. He had retreated to that place he went whenever he turned over on his side, away from her.

She thought about going to the door and saying, "Go away." She thought about going to the door, opening it and telling him that he was not welcome here. But that was unthinkable. Both those ideas were poor ones. Worst of all would be to open the door, because then that man, upset as he was, would surely barge right in, and, and good lord, maybe take Peter away.

For the first time, Tess felt the chill of fear in her limbs. She held Peter tighter.

"I'm going to get the manager, Peter, and a locksmith or

a court order or whatever I need to get in there and get you out. You don't know what's good for you anymore. One last time, boy. Open up."

In one burst of energy, Peter jumped out of bed so fast that Tess cracked her chin on his shoulder. He ran to the door and began screaming. "Get out of here, old man. Get out of here and leave us alone. You don't know what I want, you don't know what's good for me, you can't live my life, you can't even live your own life. Well, I'm telling you. Just..." he began to cry, "...just leave us alone."

"Son...." The voice came soft through the door. "Peter, just open the door and let me look at you. Let me see that you're all right. You're my only boy, you're my only flesh and blood. I love you, son, I just love you so goddamned much, I miss you and I hate this, Peter, please open the door."

Tess drew her knees up to her chin and wrapped the sheet around her. She could see the apartment door from the foot of the bed. Peter stood, head hanging, in front of the door. It looked as though he might open it. He looked broken. She saw him shudder as the sobs hicced through him.

"Peter, please."

Peter whirled around and looked at Tess. Then he fell to his knees and held his hands up in prayer to her. Her heart broke as she saw this man in such agony, such turmoil. She didn't know what to do. She smiled and blew him a kiss. Peter put his head on the floor and pounded his fists.

"Peter?" The voice came softly in. "Peter, please. Let's just talk."

Peter looked up at Tess, and he was smiling. Then he put his head down again and did a somersault. He stood up and shadow-boxed at the wall, and then slammed his hand against the door. "Get out of here, and don't come back or I'll call the cops. I hate you and I don't want anything to do with you. Ever again."

Tess gasped at the severity of his words. That was his father out there.

"Son, please." The voice was soft. And sad.

"Get out." Peter slammed on the door once more with his hand and then ran back and hopped into bed with Tess. He pulled the covers over both of their heads and entwined his legs with hers. "Know what?"

Tess was speechless.

"You answered my prayers." And then he hugged her until she hurt and she tried to be delighted at his devotion to her over his family, but she couldn't quite get the pain of his father's voice out of her memory.

* * *

Peter startled awake. He sat up in bed and wiped at a stinging drop of sweat that slipped down his nose into his eye.

The apartment was silent; Tess was breathing quietly, curled up at the bottom of the bed. Peter could hear his heart beat. He stretched. His muscles ached from disuse. His arms hurt, his legs hurt, his back hurt, his neck hurt. Even his butt hurt.

He slipped back down into the cozy warm place where

he'd been sleeping, punched up his pillow and slid it under the side of his head. And then he remembered the dream. His legs twitched.

He sat up again, not wanting to go back there, not wanting to dream about his father. He crossed his legs in front of himself, and rubbed his hands over his face, again and again, as if he could rub off his identity by rubbing off his features.

But the dream lingered.

Maybe if I can remember the entire thing—recreate it, so to speak, it will fade away.

It started with his father knocking on the door. Peter opened the door and there stood his father, with his arm around Tess. But Tess was in his bed, wasn't she? He turned and looked into the bedroom. Tess was there, but she was a hollow skeleton, thin, worn out, pale, and the Tess on his father's arm was rich and vibrant, with glossy hair and rosy cheeks. "Come with us, Peter," his father had said, and Peter tried to slam the door in his face, but Tess held the door open with one finger. He pushed and pushed, but couldn't get the door closed on their healthy faces and he knew that if he looked in the mirror, he would see a corpse of some kind.

"Come with us, Peter," Tess said, but he knew he was too sick, too diseased, too far gone to go back into the health. It would take too much work and he was too tired.

"Go with him, Princess," he said to Tess, and her eyes grew large and liquid and she let him close the door. He locked it, and the dream slid from Technicolor to black and white. He went back into the bedroom, where a thin, frail waif with brittle bones waited. "Smiggles and slunch," she said to him, and she began to laugh. She laughed hard and long, her teeth growing, her mouth enlarging until there was nothing to her but a large, loud, laughing mouth, dry and sticky, and he backed up, backed away, wondering what the fuck he was doing here, when he banged the back of his head on the wall and woke up.

Jesus.

It means nothing, he thought. It's just one of those stupid old dreams that mean nothing. Just a nightmare. Somebody once said that people had to sleep so the mind could clean house once a day, and dreams were the mind taking out the garbage. That's all that was. Garbage.

But the sweat that was beginning to dry made him feel damp and clammy and he wanted to be held, to be touched, he wanted to look into the mirror and see that he was all right.

He reached down and touched Tess. Her skin was smooth and silky to his touch. She felt marvelous. She moaned in her sleep and turned toward him, and he gathered her up in his arms and brought her back to the head of the bed where she snuggled up to him without even waking.

She's a lucky woman, he thought, and he noticed that his penis had grown hard. It had been a while. He turned her around and slid inside from the back. She awoke slowly, softly, and they rocked together for a mild eternity.

*   *   *

Arnie sat on the floor in the hallway outside Peter's apartment door for a long time. He was stunned. Paralyzed.

Overcome.

Peter had gone mad, and it was Arnie's fault. He should have seen it coming. He would have seen it coming if he hadn't been mired in his own grief and loneliness. He should have stuck with his boy a little closer. He should have been more of a father to him, during this period of double grief, more of a pal. More of a mother, too, maybe.

Arnie thought about the last time he'd talked with Peter. Peter had been holed up in there for over a month, maybe months by now, getting sicker and sicker.

Had he said "we?" He had a woman in there with him. Oh. Maybe it wasn't a woman at all. Maybe it was another boy, or a man. Maybe that was why he'd been hiding.

Arnie's head reeled. His stomach churned. He slowly stood up and made it to the elevator. He pressed the button, then turned and looked at the apartment door once more as if it had something to say to him. He hated to leave. He wanted to be with Peter. He wanted to help him.

He didn't want Peter to leave him out here all alone.

Back at home, Arnie began removing Fran. He took her picture from his dresser, took the pictures down from the walls. "I've got to get on with my life," he kept saying. "I've got to get on with it." He took the curtains she'd made down from the rods in the kitchen, and gathered up all the frilly little touches she'd put in the dining room. It all went into a plastic garbage sack. When the sack was full, he tried to close it, tried to lift it, but it was too heavy. He dragged it out through the kitchen into the garage, and set it by the trunk of the car. When he was finished, he'd put it all in the trunk and take it away.

He went back into the kitchen, and there were the plates on the walls that Fran had collected. He took them down. There were the dishtowels she'd bought. He remembered when she brought them home. They had dancing mushrooms on them. She'd loved dancing mushrooms ever since Fantasia. He grabbed them up. And the linoleum she'd picked out. And the color of blue she'd chosen on the walls. Fran was all over this house, in this house, Fran was this house.

Arnie sat in a kitchen chair and set the plates and towels on the table. He was out of control, he knew it. He knew it. He'd lost Fran, he'd lost Peter, and he didn't know what to do. He didn't know where to go. He needed something, but he didn't know what. There wasn't even a friend he could call. He didn't even have any friends.

Was that true? During all those years, didn't he and Fran make a few friends?

She had lots of friends. He got along okay with their husbands, but there was no one to whom he could pour out his pain.

No one. No one except Peter, and Peter didn't want to hear it. Peter had his own pain.

The first sobs hurt with the dryness. But finally tears came and his nose began to run, and the crying was much easier.

APRIL

Tess sat up on the edge of the bed, wishing for the first time in a long time, that she could slip into a warm flannel robe and slippers. Living nude was tiresome. Peter said they were born nude and nude was the natural way to live, but Tess thought that before they were born in all their nudity, they were nourished in a nice, warm womb. Peter said that clothes meant separateness, and she knew it would hurt his feelings if she wore any, so she just gave up on the subject.

She stood up, then waited while the blackness swirled through her vision. She'd grown accustomed to it. When it passed, she walked toward the door.

"Where?"

"Bathroom."

"No," Peter whined.

"Yes."

"Me, too."

"Come, then."

He followed her into the bathroom like a puppy and sat on the edge of the tub while she sat on the toilet. He put his elbows on his knees and his chin on his hands and watched her every move. When she finished, she stood and waited for him. But he just stood and waited with her. He apparently didn't have to go to the toilet, he just wanted to be next to her.

Exasperated, she went back to the bedroom, and opened a fresh beer.

"Peter?"

"Hmmm?" He was in bed next to her, cuddling up to her, trying to match parts of his skin to hers.

"You're too close."

He moved back.

"I mean always."

He sat up, his movements jerky. He was deeply offended. She slowly inched her way to a sitting position with the pillow behind her head and sipped her beer, then turned and looked at him.

His face was frozen like a plastic mask. She saw incredulity there, and hurt. Disbelief. But mostly hurt. When he saw that she saw, he turned his face away from her, crossed his arms over his chest, then slowly sank down onto the bed and turned on his side, away from her.

Panic flushed through Tess. She sat immobilized, considering what she had said to him, to Peter, to her love, her life. She had rejected him, she had cut him out, she had turned him away, she had closed herself off to him in a way that he didn't deserve.

But damn, she thought, enough togetherness is enough. That bit with the bathroom was just too much. It's over the line. I've got to have a little privacy, even if it is only two minutes on the toilet.

So there are limits to your love, she could hear him say. There are limits to your commitment to this experiment. There are private pockets in Candyland where bacteria can grow, where disease and dis-ease can be nurtured. Those pockets must be opened, flushed out, aired out, if this is to work.

She should have talked about it to him. Instead of snapping at him, she should have talked it out with him. Told him of her problems, her needs. He would have made them all go away, he would have understood, and listened.

But they didn't talk any more. They "communicated." With hardly any words at all. She had to think hard to choose the right word and then it was never enough. That was the point of language after all, trying to explain ideas, and the inadequacies of that language fostered metaphors and expanding illustrations, and that was the stuff of creativity. If Peter and Tess were no longer talking, then they weren't being creative. They were godless.

She hadn't even tried to explain her need for solitude to him. She had snapped at him and she may have damaged him, she may have damaged what they had together. A new panic gripped her. There may have been serious damage done. And what if? And then what? What if he threw her out? What if he left? Oh, God. She slid down into the bed and cuddled up to Peter's back. "Petie?"

He was unmoving, unresponsive.

"Sorry, Peter. Terrible sorry. Soul sorry."

"Die," he said.

"Please no, Petie, please, love you so."

She reached for his penis, but he slapped her hand away. Tears of remorse, of anger at herself, of fear that she'd ruined everything flooded out and she turned her back to him and sobbed.

When exhaustion forced her silence, she laid quietly, her pillow cold and wet, and watched as dusk entered the room. The bedroom smelled different, it didn't smell cozy and filled with love any more. It smelled angry and distrustful.

Godless.

Peter moved. She turned over and looked at him.

"Peter?"

"Kitchen," he said, and his voice was music to her ears.

"Me, too."

"Come, then."

Her heart leaped and she jumped out of bed, took hesitant steps through the blackness of her vision and then followed him, like a puppy dog, to the refrigerator.

She dared not ask him if he forgave her. Instead, she stood by his side and helped him as he loaded up two bowls with ice cream, cookies and chocolate chips. She watched and helped and wished for a big plate of steamed vegetables with a little shredded cheese on top, lightly dressed with an herby Italian. But she took her bowl of ice cream back to the bedroom where they snuggled up and ate in silence.

When things seemed to be back to normal, she ventured forth.

"Peter?"

"Hmm?"

"Forgive?"

"No."

Tears flashed to her eyes. "No?"

He took another bite of his ice cream and then turned and looked her deeply in the eyes. "No," he said.

"Well, I'm sorry, Peter," she said, feeling her face flushed. "We don't ever talk any more. It seems like there is a lot for us to discuss, but we don't talk. How can I tell you how I feel if we don't talk?"

He just kept his gaze level. This was the most she'd said in a month.

"How can you tell me how you feel?" she asked.

"You know."

"Well, maybe you're better at this than I am."

"Try."

"I am trying. I have been trying."

"More."

"I've got to have a vehicle of some kind...an outlet."

She sat up on her knees, put her ice cream on the bed, faced him and put her chilled hands on his chest. "Peter, please, I'm so afraid of destroying us. But I need...I don't know what."

Peter took her hands and kissed each palm. Then he rolled over on his side, away from her, and for a moment, she felt lost and alone. Then she saw that he'd picked up the telephone and was dialing.

Notebooks and pens were delivered the next morning, along with corn chips, clam dip, popcorn and a big bag of M&Ms.

Peter wrote at the top of her red spiral bound, "To my Contessa. Be still."

Tess wrote at the top of his blue spiral bound, "To Peter, my love."

And then they both began to write in their own notebooks.

Tess found she had no sour words for Peter, only words of love and devotion, and of how hard it was to accept someone exactly the way he was, yet knowing that this was the only way to total achievement of absolute oneness. She tried, she tried to be one with him, and she wrote of her feelings and the physical sensations that accompanied this exertion. The words fell out of the end of her pen so fast she could barely keep up with them. This was a catharsis of the most exquisite kind.

And when she was finished, she had filled up four pages of tightly spaced writing. She felt better than she had in a long time. This made her feel the way her orgasms used to make her feel.

She closed her book, snuggled up to Peter and kissed him. "Read?" he asked.

Her first reaction was no, this is private, I never thought we'd share these things. Then she remembered that the purpose of their life was to achieve the oneness, and there was nothing to hide because Peter had all the same thoughts, he knew what was in her book anyway. She had to let him read it just because he asked. She quickly reviewed what she wrote to see if there was anything damaging in it, and then she smiled and handed it to him.

He handed his to her, and she kissed it and then opened it and there was a drawing of a praying mantis on the first page.

And nothing else.

Its triangular head was cocked to look at her with its bulbous eyes, its hooked claws poised and ready for some victim.

Praying mantises ate their mates. The females bit the heads off their mates during copulation, and while the mindless nerve center of the male kept right on humping, humping, breeding her in thoughtless, pleasureless, oblivious instinct, the female just calmly ate his brain.

Tess was astonished at Peter's talent for drawing. It would have been magnificent in charcoal or even pencil, where he could have shaded its wings and really made the eyes look alive. With a blue ball-point pen, it had more of a comic-book look. Even so, it was quite a piece of work.

But what did it mean?

She looked at him. He was busy reading what she'd written. She watched his eyes go back and forth across the page, trying to read something in his face, some message to her that said that he approved of her writing, or disapproved, something that would tell her how to act when he'd finished. Maybe she could also find something in his face that would tell her what he meant by drawing that insect—the first thing in his new book. Was there a symbolism there? How can we possibly have the same thoughts when I can't figure him out at all?

He finished and looked up over the top of the notebook at her. There was no expression in his face at all. None.

He closed the book and put it down on his lap, then he slid it over to her side of the bed and turned over on his side, away from her.

"Peter?"

"Hmm?"

"Don't go." She rubbed his side, his hip, his leg, but he ignored her. Eventually, she stopped, and picked at her cuticles. His notebook was open, and the face of that creature stared out at her. "Devoted to you, Peter," she said, then turned over on her side, away from him, and soon fell asleep.

When she awoke, he was busy drawing again, this time in her red book. She had a feeling of possessiveness, a little resentment that he would be so presumptuous as to commandeer her book. It was hers, after all, not his. He could draw objectionable things in his own book, but not in hers. She wanted to snatch it away from him, but instead, she just watched him. He saw that she was awake, and blew her a kiss. Then he went back to his work.

The kiss soothed her. She snuggled down in the covers and watched his hand move across the page. She watched his head tilt this way and that as he observed the artwork taking form —he seemed to be pleased with what he was doing— but still she didn't know what it was. He worked for a long time, and she just watched, silent, contented.

And then he finished. She knew it because he sighed, and then relaxed. He put his pen on the nightstand and closed the book. Tess put out her hand and he handed it to her. She looked at his face, but again, there was no expression. She smiled at him and then opened her book.

It was a picture of her in profile. Her freckles, her stupid little snub nose, her curls—they almost looked red.

But there was more. She wore a flimsy kind of tunic, and her tiny little breasts poked their little nipples through the fabric, but in back...in back, giant gossamer wings were gently folded in rest.

An angel. Peter had drawn her as an angel. Tears sprang to her eyes, tears of happiness, joy, and she was so glad, so grateful to be here. She snuggled down next to him and farther down, and farther down, and she took his penis in her mouth while he lay back, hands behind his head, and she loved him as best she knew how.

It was pitch black when Tess awoke. Peter jerked and writhed next to her. She sat up and looked down on him. In the dim light shining in from the bedroom window, she could see perspiration standing out on his face and his chest. His eyes moved beneath the lids and his face jerked back and forth, back and forth as if he were denying something, denying everything.

Fascinated, Tess slowly pulled the sheet off him, and watched the muscles in his body flex and slack with his nightmare. She watched as he began an erection, and then it deflated as if punctured. She watched perspiration drip down and collect in the smooth white scar on his hip. He shuddered, his mouth opened and then closed, forming great round words that had no sound. His feet danced.

She wiped the droplets of sweat from the scar with her forefinger. She touched his belly, smoothed the dampness from the hair that grew from his chest down toward his navel. Still he dreamed.

She scooted over, and then straddled him. She could see his sleep settle a bit, and then it began again, his violent motions as he tried to sweep away the horrors of the night.

He was unsuccessful.

She was horrified, in a way, that he had to be terrorized in his sleep, and in another way she was pleased that something tortured him in much the same way that he occasionally tortured her. She liked this torture of him because she was totally blameless. She wanted to know what it was that haunted his dreams, but knew he would never tell.

So she sat on him, watching him, watching this person he had become, thin, white, hounded, haunted. She sat on him and she wished she knew him better.

* * *

Peter awoke with a lurch and sat up in bed. He felt cold and damp, the moist, smelly sheets wrapped around him like a rotting shroud.

It was daylight—he could see the sun coming in around the edges of the shade—but in the bedroom, it was perpetually dusk.

He ached all over; he felt as though he hadn't had a good night's sleep in years.

Tess was sleeping peacefully next to him, a thin forearm thrown over her eyes. Her hair had been brushed.

So she'd been up already this morning. She'd brushed her hair, probably her teeth, gone to the toilet.

What else had she done while he was asleep? What else had she done, what other separatist task had she committed, that he didn't know about, that he couldn't know about?

He looked around the room. The phone cord lay strewn in a lazy S on the carpet. The last time he looked at it, he recalled, it had been neatly coiled. Had Tess used the telephone this morning? Who had she called? What had they talked about?

Peter felt his heart pound. He looked at her again. He seemed to remember something about her in the middle of the night, something about having to look up to her, something about her having power over him. Maybe she'd called someone about him. Maybe she called his father.

What would she have said?

He reached over and pinched a bit of the skin on her side. He squeezed hard. She jumped, her eyes flew open, and she rubbed the reddening spot. "Ow."

She looked guilty. She definitely looked guilty.

She looked at him questioningly, and he just stared at her, willing her to confess. She would, too, she would confess. She couldn't keep such a terrible secret from him, not now, at least, not now that he was on to her game.

She rubbed her side and looked at him with feigned innocence and wondering. He just watched her, waiting for her to hang herself with the rope he was giving her.

* * *

Arnie sat in front of the telephone, a letter and its ripped-open envelope next to it. The letter was from his supervisor's supervisor at work. It said, in part, that if he didn't show up for work or call with a physician's excuse within forty-eight hours, that his termination check would be sent to him.

He'd taken his two weeks, and another two weeks, and more after that. He'd just not showed. And now the letter, and no matter how hard he tried, he couldn't lift that blasted telephone receiver to call the office and tell them he wouldn't be coming in any more. Or grovel for his job. Or tell them all to go to hell. He couldn't do it. He couldn't call them. They had no idea what was going on in his world, in his family, in his mind. They had no idea at all. None of them had a son holed up.

Peter.

Arnie slammed his hand down on the tabletop, and the stinging brought him back to life. Peter.

Arnie just didn't know what to try next.

He'd been back to Noble's office to make sure he heard right the first time. The deli delivered food to Peter's apartment once, twice, three times a week. Had since December. December! Arnie had looked at the receipts. Candy and beer. Candy and beer. Candy and beer. What the hell was going on with those two?

He went to the deli and talked to the delivery boy. The boy said a girl usually answered the door, but he never saw her, because he had to leave the groceries outside.

Arnie was relieved to find out that Peter was shacking up with a girl, but that didn't explain....

The phone rang and Arnie almost jumped right out of his skin. He looked at it for a long time. Fran used to let the phone ring sometimes while she was sitting right in front of it. "My phone," she'd say. "I pay the bill, it's there for my convenience. I don't want to talk to anybody right now. If it's important, they'll call back."

Arnie never understood that until now. He looked at the phone and thought perhaps he wouldn't answer it.

But what if it was Peter? What if he needed help?

He picked up the receiver and held it to his ear. "Hello?" His voice sounded phlegmy and clogged. He hadn't spoken aloud to anyone in a long time.

"Hello, Arnie? This is Leesha." Leesha. Across the street. "You know, Leesha? Across the street?"

"Hi, Leesha."

"You're not going to work anymore. I mean, I couldn't help but notice. Is everything all right?"

"Yeah." Arnie cleared his throat. "I'm just on a kind of extended leave right now."

"Oh. Well, listen, I wondered if you'd be interested in a movie tonight. There's a good one over at the mall, and I'm going to go, although I kind of hate going by myself. If you're by yourself tonight, maybe we could just kind of go to the movie together. You know?"

"I can't tonight, Leesha."

"Oh? Got a date already?"

"No, I'm just kind of...I don't feel very...not tonight, Leesha."

"When Mickey died, Arnie, I went into a blue funk so deep I thought I'd die, and so did everybody else around me." The shy little girl act was gone. "You've got to get out, Arnie, I mean it. I'll pick you up at seven."

"No, Leesha..."

"I won't take no for an answer. See you then." She hung up.

I should never have answered it, he thought.

Leesha and Mickey were a notch above acquaintances. Their kids were a little bit younger than Peter, but they all played together when they were little. The four parents got together at various functions, and once or twice they got together for a barbecue and a game of Scrabble, but there was never much chemistry among them. When Mickey died a few years ago in a car accident, Fran spent some time over there with Leesha, and that had been the last of it.

A date with Leesha. Arnie never thought much of her. She always had that little girl act, something that some men found attractive, but Arnie did not. Fran was a woman—a grown woman, with a woman's tastes and feelings. Arnie liked that.

But a movie date, well, that was perhaps something different. A movie might be a good thing.

And then he realized he had not thought of Peter for maybe ten minutes. Ten whole minutes. Yes, he thought, maybe a movie with Leesha is just exactly what I need.

*   *   *

She was right on time, wearing miniature jeans and a casual purple cotton sweater. Her hair was blonder, and she wore it up with one of those purple things that made a vertical ponytail. Her bangs were curled and blonde and she wore pearl earrings. She looked terrific.

Arnie had managed to change his clothes, wash his face and comb his hair, but he wasn't exactly sure when he last showered or did any laundry.

She drove to the mall, chattering away the whole time. Arnie looked out the window, not thinking of Peter, exactly, not thinking of much of anything. Numb. As numb as he had ever been, even when Fran died.

The movie was nothing special, and they had pie and ice cream afterwards, Leesha holding up the date all by herself. By the end of the evening, Arnie was filled with admiration for the woman who was willing to go through this for a stranger, practically.

She drove them back, parked the car in her driveway. "Want to come in?"

"Naah," he said, which was about all he had said all evening. It sounded whiny and stupid to him. "Well, okay." That sounded better. He didn't want to be this way, it just seemed to be the way he was right now.

"Good."

Her house was immaculate. She began with the chatter about the house as soon as they walked into the living room. She went to the kitchen while he sank into the sofa, and she returned with glasses of wine.

"Arnie?" She sat down next to him and handed him his wine. He wanted to drink it straight down.

"Hmm?" He sipped, glad he hadn't gone home to his empty house. Not quite yet.

"Would you like to spend the night?"

The question took him right off guard. He looked down at her. There was much to this woman he had never noticed before. She called him, asked him out, entertained him all evening, and now was willing to throw him a mercy fuck. Well, she'd been right on so far. She had provided everything he needed, especially since he had no idea what he needed. "I'd like that very much," he said.

She smiled at him and clinked her glass with his.

The bedroom, he found, had been redone in frilliness. He'd been in this bedroom before, putting a sleeping Peter down on their bed when he was little, and it had been a sensible couples-type bedroom then. Now it seemed like something out of a catalog. And he felt like a plastic mannequin.

Leesha excused herself and went into the bathroom.

Arnie sat on the edge of the bed and took off his shoes, feeling awkward and highly visible. He turned out the light, then shucked the rest of his clothes and slipped between the sheets. They were cool and smooth. It made him want to get clean sheets—or at least wash the ones that were on his bed.

Leesha opened the bathroom door, clicked off the light, and then slipped in next to him.

This was so different. She was so different from Fran, this bed felt different, the room felt different. He wondered for a moment if he was dreaming.

Then Leesha was snuggling up next to him, and it was no dream, but it had been over twenty-five years since he'd been with a woman other than Fran, and the differences staggered him.

"We can just snuggle up and go to sleep, Arnie. I mean, we don't have to do anything, you know? Unless you want to, and that would be okay, too."

"I do," he said, partly out of obligation, and he ran his hand over her smooth skin, down over the roundness of her hip, back over her tiny butt, up her spine to her shoulder. She felt wonderful, but the heat and the desire that should have come up didn't. He kissed her throat and fondled her breast. He'd almost forgotten what a woman felt like.

But still his loins didn't stir to life.

Soon her hands were upon him, and the lack of interest his body felt was all too apparent. He snorted in frustration. She gently pushed him back on the bed, then snuggled up into the crook of his arm.

"Don't push it, Arnie," she said. "Just sleep with me tonight."

He stared at the ceiling, and within seconds, all thought of Leesha and Mickey were gone. Instead, he was trying to figure out how to breach Peter's apartment.

MAY

Tess watched Peter watch her. At first, she thought he was drawing her portrait, he had his notebook, and the yellow number two pencils that the deli delivered, and he sat with his back against the wall, propped up with pillows, and he watched her with small, squinty eyes. He watched her and he drew.

But he didn't watch her the way he would if he were sketching her. If he were drawing a picture of her, he would be looking at her, looking at her features, her hair, her nose, the way the light came in through the shaded window, the shadows on the dark side of her face. No, Peter wasn't looking at her, he was watching her.

There was a terrible difference.

Tess curled up a little tighter on the foot of the bed and chewed the end of her pen. Every time she moved, she felt his eyes on her. They were quick, darty. Suspicious.

She drew little lines and squiggles on the page. Her words were stuck. She wanted to write so badly, she needed to write, she needed to write the truth, but she was afraid that if Peter read what she wrote, he would go on a rampage, and Peter on a rampage was not a pretty sight.

Besides, she thought as she chewed, what is the truth, really? That's exactly the problem, she reasoned. Unless I can get these words down onto paper or verbalize them in some form, I don't really know what it is that I'm trying to say.

She moved again, restless, Peter's gaze boring through her like a heat laser.

She looked up at him and he stared at her.

"Peter is sick," she wrote, and then glanced guiltily up at him. He was busy drawing. His drawings had become more and more bizarre, his nightmares had grown wild and violent, he had become more and more withdrawn. Tess wished she knew what to do for him. There were two conflicting opinions deep inside her. One was that his spirit was growing at a magnificent rate and he needed space in order to do that. He would break though to the other side any day now and be a higher spiritual being, more centered and aware and wise than any other on this planet at this time. He might even be the new Messiah. Extraordinary growth requires extraordinary nourishment. This was what Tess wanted to believe. This is what Peter wanted her to believe.

The other voice inside her said that Peter was terribly ill, that he needed help, needed it badly, needed it now. This was the small voice that came to Tess in the quiet time before and after sleep; it begged her to help him. She wrestled with ideas of how she could help him, but came up empty. I could never take him anywhere, she thought, I could never call someone in for him.

And then, the Great Compromise formed within her. I can nurse him myself, she thought, I can heal him, if only I can believe strongly enough. We are the yin and the yang, we are God together. Together we can do this thing, it'll be all right. And that way, just in case he turned out to be the great spiritual leader he thought he would be, she was safe. She had not betrayed him. She was no Judas.

It didn't matter which idea was correct, they were both bad. If Peter were a Chosen One, what would he want with her, once he got his calling? He would either cast her aside, and she would fade into nothingness, or he would use her until she had nothing else to give—already he was light years ahead of her in terms of brilliance.

Either way, she lost.

And if he were going mad? Well, she would lose him that way, too, but at least she could live with herself. She would stand by him, loyal to the end. At least she could be with him, help him, love him... Hadn't her Sunday school teacher talked about the power of love the same way Peter had? Surely they could work this thing through.

And, who's to say she wasn't almost as mad as he?

The compromise stood.

"He needs me," she finally wrote, and felt complete.

Tess knew it had been a few days since they'd showered. The sheets looked dingy and limp and she could smell herself. She scampered up the bed toward Peter and said, "Now?"

"No," he said, and pulled his drawing pad toward him so she couldn't see it.

"Now."

"No."

"When?"

He just stared at her.

It was time for him to take the leftover rotting food, the candy wrappers, the crumbs and trash into the kitchen while she showered. Then she would change the sheets while he showered. It was time.

"I'm going," she said, and got up. He watched her with that strange squinty expression, as she walked around the bed.

She turned the shower water on full force and hot. It needled into her skin and she loved it. It felt wonderful. She soaped up, hair, face, throat, arms, legs, crotch, and then rinsed off, feeling her curly hair rinse out long and straight and luxurious. It felt wonderful. Then she turned off the water, got a big towel and dried off, seeing her ribs through her fragile, blue-veined skin, seeing her hip bones, that horrible scar between them, noticing how thin her arms and legs had become. She dried her feet and straightened up a little too fast, and the blackness swirled about her vision. She groped for the shower curtain, and then sat down on the toilet until the blackness passed. When it did, she felt weak. Showering was a big job these days. She stood slowly and wiped the mirror clean.

Her face had grown old. Sunken and hollow. Yellowish.

She toweled her hair, thought maybe some orange juice would be good, wrapped the towel around her and opened the bathroom door.

Peter stood there, leaning against the jamb. His scowl made her shrink back from him. He tore the towel away from her and threw it on the ground. "You closed the door," he said, "and dressed."

She was speechless. He was accusing her of doing something that came almost naturally, it came so naturally she didn't give it a second thought. She didn't know why she'd closed the bathroom door, it was something she'd done all her life, even when she lived alone, she closed the bathroom door, and now it was a crime. And dressed? She wrapped a warm, damp towel around herself to walk into the chilly air of the apartment.

But she'd never done either of those things here before. She shrugged her shoulders.

In the bedroom, she saw that he'd not taken off the soiled sheets, nor had he removed the candy wrappers and donut boxes. She began to gather them up. Peter watched from the doorway.

"Go shower."

"Why?"

"Smell bad."

He got that squinty-eyed look again, reached down and unplugged the telephone. He wrapped the cord around the phone and took it with him to the bathroom and slammed the door behind him.

"He is sick," she said to herself and began to strip the bed. When he came back, he had not dried off at all. He dripped on the carpeting; rivulets coursed from his wet hair all down his back. He limped, she saw, and the wide silver scar on his hip had grown thin along with the rest of his physique. He still held the phone in his hand and it, too, was wet, as if he'd not let it go at all while he showered.

She put the sheets in the washer and turned it on. She got fresh sheets from the closet and brought them back into the bedroom. Peter stood still, looking down at his notebook, which was on the floor.

"You peeked," he said.

"Peeked? At your drawings? No, I didn't."

"You did."

Tess snapped open the bottom sheet and shook it out on the bed. She began to tuck in the corners. With apparent reluctance, Peter helped. Then she gathered up all the rest of the food trash around the bed and took it into the kitchen.

"Trash out."

"No," he said, and plugged in the telephone.

She just looked at him. He was being an ornery child today. The garbage chute was two doors down at the end of the hallway. Peter had only to wrap a towel around himself and walk the brown paper sack of garbage down to it, open the door, toss it in and come back. He'd done it every time it needed to be done before.

She picked up the brown paper sack, carried it to the other side of the kitchen and leaned it up against the wall.

"This garbage will come back to haunt you," she said, then walked past him to the bedroom.

He stood there for a long time, staring at the sack of trash. Then he slowly walked into the kitchen and regarded it from all angles.

"Haunt?" he finally said.

"Yes, Peter, haunt. That trash will haunt you."

"Curse?"

"Yes, Peter, old, smelly, moldy garbage is a curse."

He stood there, his face growing redder and it looked as if he wanted to speak, wanted to scream and shout, but instead he clenched his fists and his teeth and stood there, trembling.

"Talk to me, Peter," she said gently. "Let's not play this game anymore. C'mon. Please. Tell me."

"No!" He grabbed his notebook and his pencil and sat on the floor, drawing, scribbling furiously. "Don't—curse—me," he said, the words coming hard and tight as he worked.

Tess sat up in bed, watching him. He worked with a fury that was matched only by that of his nightmares. Perspiration stood out on his forehead. She saw it trickle down his sides as he drew, one large vein standing out on his forehead. This is good for him, she thought. He needs to get his emotions down on paper. It is part of what he wants to do. It is what he needs to do.

She watched him work, his pencil scratching furiously into the paper, and Tess knew that he was creating a masterpiece. She was reminded of the passion of the artists, and this was it, right before her eyes.

I hardly know this man, she thought.

Yet she loved him with her entire being.

The phone rang.

Peter's body jerked in response, and his pencil fell silent.

The phone rang again.

Slowly, he raised his head and looked at her, that squinty expression back again. He was accusing her of something, but she didn't know what.

The phone rang again, insistent, interrupting, jarring, rude.

"Answer it," he said.

Tess couldn't believe what she was hearing. "No."

"Answer it, damn you. It's for you."

"For me?" Tess sat back on her heels, not comprehending. "It's not for me, Peter."

He stared at her while the phone rang again and again and again and again. Sixteen times, twenty times, it was the longest it had ever run unanswered, and Tess knew that it was Peter's father. Peter twitched every time it rang.

"Garbage!" he jumped up, ran into the kitchen. Tess heard him pick up the bag of trash, open the door and run out with it.

The phone rang.

She heard the door to the garbage chute slam closed.

The phone rang.

Then Peter was back, shutting, bolting and chaining the door. He'd gone out into the hall naked.

Tess tensed for the next ring of the telephone. There wasn't one. It had stopped.

"Curse, you said," Peter walked to her, stood next to the

bed, tall, huge, menacing. "You cursed it."

Then he picked up his pencil from the floor, knelt on the bed, pushed her out of the way and scribbled a thick line down the middle of the bed with his pencil.

She was to stay on her side of the bed, that was clear.

He fetched his notebook from the floor, turned the page, and began to draw again, only this time he seemed cold, calculating, his lines heavy and slow, methodical. He was drawing something that was full of hard lines and angles. There was no heated passion here, Tess thought. If this was passion, it was frigid.

In the middle of the night, Tess awoke. She didn't jar awake, or hear something that spooked her, she just awoke, and she woke fully aware. She lay quietly, eyes open. She could see the line Peter had drawn on the sheet, she could smell the graphite.

Peter. Something had turned in him, something rare was coming out. It was part of the experiment, Tess knew, but she didn't know how far Peter was taking it—was he joking with this "curse" stuff, or did he really mean for her to stay on one half of the bed? Was he toying with her mind, or testing her fidelity, her dedication to their togetherness? How was she shaping up? She'd had such sinful thoughts about him being sick, about him needing help, separatist thoughts.

She moved around a little bit, scratched her nose, turned the pillow over.

As she did, she saw Peter, sitting up, head resting against the wall, staring at her.

In the dim light, his eyes shone like little steel balls as he sat there, wide awake, staring at her.

Tess's blood ran cold. He couldn't be playing at some of this stuff. What should she do? He'd die if she called someone. He would. He would refuse to eat, he would separate himself from life and just die, she knew it. She knew the kind of will he had. No, they would turn him into an animal in an institution. It was up to her to help him.

She wished he would just will himself to the other side. She wished he would just flash and be gone. Instantly. He could do it, she was sure. She knew the power of his will.

"Peter?"

Silence.

"Peter, please talk to me."

"You. Sabotage."

"Me? No, no, no, I'm not." She sat up, bringing the sheet up with her. She pulled her knees up underneath her and leaned against the wall, holding the sheet to cover her front. In the face of groundless accusations, she suddenly felt too nude, too vulnerable.

He grabbed the sheet and ripped it from her grasp.

"Who did you call?"

"Call? Me? Nobody."

"Liar."

Tess was speechless.

"You cursed the garbage and made the phone ring."

"No, Peter, you're wrong."

"You're wrong. I hate you."

"Peter, listen to me. Something is happening here, something not good, something not healthy. You have to talk to me, you have to listen to me, you have to write out your feelings. Write out your fears."

"Stupid."

"Not stupid. Please, Peter, we're making the experiment, right? We're creating. We're our own Gods in our own universe, yes?"

"God must have Satan. You."

"Oh, Peter, please don't do this to me. I love you so much, I want us to be happy and serene and filled with love and life...." Tess choked and began to cry. Life felt hopeless. She sank down, picked up a pillow and hugged it to her.

Peter grabbed the pillow away from her, grabbed her thin shoulders with his hands and threw her down. He pried her legs apart and she saw he had an enormous erection. He thrust deeply into her, and she yelled, it hurt, it rasped, it wasn't nice, it wasn't gentle, it wasn't loving, and he picked up her hips with his hands, bending her head forward until her chin was on her chest and he rammed her and rammed her and rammed her, bruising her deeply, and she cried and pleaded, but he kept on, not seeing, not hearing, not knowing anything she said.

When he finished, he rolled her over onto her side of the bed. He unplugged the telephone, wrapped the cord around it and put it in the bottom drawer of his nightstand. Then he got up and left, closing the bedroom door behind him.

Tess was stunned. The hurt was too deep to realize.

Her tears dried up as she lay there, wondering about Peter, wondering about herself, wondering why she wasn't up and out of there in a flash. He had no call to treat her like that.

But it was part of the experiment.

She could hear Peter puking in the bathroom.

That was even more important than the fact that he'd just raped her. She picked up her journal and began to write, then thought better of it. Code, she thought. I need a code, because if I write the truth and Peter doesn't like it, or agree with it, or wants to change it, then the record will be all for naught. And it is time that this thing—this experiment, this experience—be recorded. In its entirety. From beginning to end. I need a code. Something simple.

She wrote the alphabet at the top of the page and then began to write her journal entry, substituting each letter for the letter following it in the alphabet. Peter became Qfufs. It worked. It was clumsy and slow, but she managed it.

Peter came back from the bathroom, his face flushed and damp. Without speaking, he got into bed, turned on his side away from her, and soon he slept.

Tess kept writing, a sense of the importance of her words growing. She wrote until the sky lightened.

* * *

When Peter awoke, Tess was sleeping, her pen still in her hand, her journal tossed to the side. Gently, so as not to wake her, he took it and sat up. He opened it, anxious to read what she had said about him.

But it was in a foreign language. He never knew that Tess

knew a foreign language.

His blood chilled. It was even worse than he thought. In addition to making calls in the middle of the night, she was writing secrets, keeping secrets from him. Writing secrets about him. He looked at her sleeping there, her face thin and pale. Her wrists were so thin he could break them in his grasp, he thought, he could crush her so easily, break her up, kill her. He could kill her so easily, and nobody would miss her

Nobody would ever miss her.

He flexed his fingers. It would feel good, he thought. It would feel really good to break something, to just squeeze something until it broke or quit or died. He felt the muscles in his forearms respond to the idea.

Then Tess moved. Her brow wrinkled, her legs twitched, she rearranged herself a little bit, her lips pouted and then she relaxed.

Those movements were all familiar. He loved this woman. She was his the way no woman, no person, no thing, no... no...no nothing had ever been his before.

He couldn't hurt her, he had to protect her. She belonged to him, traitor that she was. He would just have to teach her better. She would confess to him and he would keep her safe.

* * *

"Noble? Arnie Vernon. Peter Vernon's dad."

"Arnie. How nice to hear from you."

"Noble, I'm going to need some money."

"Let's see...."

127

"I had a management contract with Peter, and money from it accumulated in my account, but I didn't need it, so I never took it. I thought someday Peter would need it, or maybe for my retirement...."

"Yes, yes, I remember. How much do you want, Arnie?"

"Maybe you could send me a thousand dollars a month."

"I'll check on that, Arnie. As I recall, that won't be a problem."

"Good. And listen, Noble, have you heard from my boy?"

"No, I haven't. I see that his account is quite active, I was reviewing his investments just last week. But I haven't seen him or heard from him in a long time."

"Yeah, well...."

"Is everything all right?"

"Sure," Arnie said. "Thanks, Noble."

"Anytime. I'll see that Marjorie cuts a check today."

Arnie hung up. There was enough money in that account to last him. The house was paid for. In fact, he should be on easy street, he and Peter both. Peter's winnings were quite good—not spectacular as pro earnings sometimes are, but they were very good. He paid off the house, bought the apartment, and the rest Noble invested and used to pay the bills.

Arnie had kept his electrician's job because he was too young and too proud to be supported by his son. He'd taken a two-year leave of absence to coach Peter, but when it was clear that Peter had outgrown Arnie's abilities, they hired a professional coach and Arnie went back to the old grind. It was familiar and comfortable, in a way.

And now he'd let the job go. Just never gone back. He supposed he'd hear from the pension people eventually, but they took a long time. In the meantime, he could get along on Noble's thousand dollars a month.

And had to try to let Peter live his own life.

That's what Leesha was trying to tell him, and he could see the wisdom in what she was saying.

Leesha. She'd been a guest in his home, in his bed, about four nights out of every seven. It was getting to be a habit for both of them. A nice habit. There was nothing serious developing—at least he didn't think there was, but the companionship was good, the sex was nice, the diversion was very important, and sometimes he even found himself laughing again.

Laughing.

And then she would destroy the mood by saying something like, "It does you good to let go a little, Arnie," and that would remind him of what it was she was trying to get him to let go of: Peter. And then the fragile, temporary shield that separated him from his worry would shatter. The familiar pressure of worry and fear pushed in on him. Automatically, he would reach for the phone, dial Peter's apartment and listen to the phone ring.

Leesha would eventually go home.

JUNE

Soon writing in code became automatic. Once Tess realized she was writing as fast in code as she could the regular way, writing became her entire life. She wrote every waking moment. Sometimes her hands would ache from the strain of it, and she would switch hands, desperate to get every word ever spoken between them, down in black and white. This was the actual record—the gospel—of Candyland, and it was important, it was so terribly important. It was her job, and she dare not take it lightly.

Night and day merged, Peter seemed even to merge into the background of her life while she caught up, writing the history, itching to get caught up to the present, so she could just record the day-to-day occurrences. She cried as she wrote, and she laughed, and there was saliva sprayed across the page, and tear drops blossoming on the ink, and smudges from her perspiration. She wrote and she wrote, the pen never moving fast enough to keep up with the torrent of emotion-packed words, and she felt as if she was doing something real for the first time in her life.

Tess looked up from her writing and Peter was staring at her in a way that told her he was confused. He was wrestling with a problem, that was clear, and he didn't know how to approach her.

All I can do, she thought, is make myself available to him. "What is it?"

His eyes opened wide in surprise, and he scooted back away from her, frightened. He picked up his journal and started to draw. She leaned closer, to look over the top of his journal, but he whipped it from her sight and glared at her. When she sat back on her own side of the bed, he again began to draw, but kept glancing in her direction to make sure she was keeping out of his way. She noted all of this in her journal.

Over the past weeks, Tess had begun to view her journal in a new way. It had become something entirely different from what she had originally intended for it. At first, it was a vehicle for catharsis, where she could pour out her heart and soul and focus her ideas. It was also a way she could share with Peter without speaking, those personal things that were too important to be spoken aloud, in front of the other's reaction. There were times in a relationship for thought before action, and when everything was spoken face-to-face, then there was no hiding, no time to think before acting, it was all immediate and irrefutable.

Peter thought that was a good idea. He thought that they should be exposed, inside and out, to each other, all their little nooks and crannies aired out and made fresh. But that didn't always work; at least it didn't for Tess. She liked the writing and the sharing, and sometimes the words on the paper were gentler than they were on the tongue, and sometimes the pictures they made were so much prettier, and sometimes it was just plain easier to write than to confront.

But then the journals began to change. Peter never wrote in his, at least not that Tess had ever noticed. He only drew. He drew wonderful pictures that ranged from seascapes and landscapes to mythological creatures and pictures of her, or whatever concept he was trying to convey. One time he drew a wonderful picture of her foot, half cloaked in wrinkled sheet, while she slept. It was wonderful. And sensuous. And she understood exactly what he wanted, and their lovemaking that time was better than it had ever been. And then Peter's pictures became darker, he used more force when drawing them, occasionally even tearing the paper with the point of the pencil. His figures turned strange, warped, like the vague monsters that spring from nightmares, and Tess found it more important to write about Peter than to write to him. She still wrote her feelings and her dreams, but the focus of her journal was Peter, and how their togetherness had changed him.

If they were gods—and Tess believed maybe they were— then her writings, punctuated with his illustrations, were the gospel.

She began to write as if her words, even more than the diary of Anne Frank, would be read and studied for generations, as a study in human development, as a characterization of the two people who chose to rise above the mundane. She wrote of Peter as being the all-powerful one, as she being his queen and consort, of his decisions and their discussions being life-changing issues. And they were. They were.

What Tess and Peter were doing in Candyland was the highest form of self-sacrifice in the face of self-indulgence.

Wasn't that the stuff of saints? The thought made her gasp. Then she smiled. It was, it was.

She thought some more about saints. They performed miracles, they did good, they did no wrong. They were on the right side of God. It all fit.

Tess and Peter fit the description, it was true.

She wrote it all down, encoded, and as she did, it became clear to her how all of her past actions, all of the things she'd said and done and heard and saw were leading up to this point. She and Peter were the only two chosen in this world, in this lifetime, perhaps in this generation, possibly in this millennium, to have this opportunity and to make the best of it.

She wrote that down, and then said, "Peter?"

He looked up from his drawing, then squinted at her.

"We're saints."

His expression did not change.

"And maybe you're the new Messiah. These," she pointed at their journals, "together, they illustrate it all, my writings and your drawings. They're the new gospel." There. She'd said it out loud, and while it sounded mildly insane, it also sounded like it could very well be the truth. Her face flushed.

Peter looked down at his drawing, and Tess could tell that she'd touched him. She was right. The truth had been revealed to her at just the perfect moment, and Peter recognized it as the truth. It was working. The Candyland experiment was working. How had she ever doubted it?

She reached over and touched his arm. He looked at her with an expression of love that she hadn't seen in months. He still loved her, he was just confused. These were confusing times. Who had a messiah manual, anyway? It was confusing, and hard and difficult and scary, but they would see it through together, the two of them.

"Together, Peter," she said.

"Contessa," he said, and then the phone rang.

Peter sat up and cleared his throat. He looked as though he was going to answer it.

"Christ," Peter said. "Kind, gentle, loving." He pointed at the phone as it rang again. "A new message." He picked up the phone and held it between them so they could both hear.

"Peter? Peter, is that you, son?"

"Hello," Peter said, his voice phlegmy and croaky.

"Oh, Peter, God, my boy, it's good to hear your voice. How are you?"

"Blessed," he said, and Tess saw a light in his eyes.

"Yes you are, son, and so am I, by God, it's good to talk to you. Listen, do you think we might get together one of these days? It's been a long time, you know, I'd really like to see you, meet your girlfriend—"

Peter's eyes flashed. He looked at Tess, and she saw the fear returning. "No," he said.

"Okay, okay, that's fine, it's good just to have you

answering the phone. Well, listen, I bought you a little something, I thought I just might drop it by the apartment."

"No! No! No!" Peter slammed the phone down. He turned to Tess and gripped her arms with ferocity. "The message, Tessa. The message—" he choked. "Crucify."

His eyes floated out of focus, he released her, pulled the covers up over him, wrapped his arms around himself and turned on his side, away from her.

She gently touched his shoulder and he shrugged away from her. "Keep drawing, Peter," she said. "This is important stuff."

She picked up her journal and began to record the event.

* * *

Don't give an inch, Peter told himself. You've already given too much. Answering the phone was a terrible mistake. It was an opportunity, it was an "in," and if that door isn't slammed shut on everybody, then they will take my soul and rip it apart in front of the whole world.

Even Tess. She doesn't know. She doesn't understand. She can't possibly know the tortures of the hunted one. It isn't her; she sometimes has glimpses of what it's all about, she takes messages for me, but she isn't in my shoes. No, he thought. She isn't in my shoes, and she could have me sacrificed without knowing it. The way Mother was sacrificed.

Martyred.

She was so good, he thought, and visions of his young mother filled his head. She was so good, so wonderful, so gentle, so warm. He saw her sitting at a tennis match, sunglasses covering her perfect eyes, hair lightly sun bleached, white sleeveless blouse showing off her tanned, muscled arms. She wore a coral colored lipstick, and she shouted when he won a point—he would look over at her, and her teeth shined white in the sun. As white as her hat, as white as her shorts.

Then she went to the hospital every day for ten days and by the time the tenth day had come her breast had split open like a ripe melon from the radiation burns and she lay on the couch, raw wound oozing, her beautiful breast, her perfect breast exposed to the air because to cover it meant excruciating pain. She didn't know he saw her; she would have shot herself in the head if she knew he'd seen her. Slowly the breast healed, the radiation burns went away, but they had burned something else out of her as well. They had burned out her life. They had burned out her soul. They had removed her soul and strung it up on a cross for everyone to see—especially him. He saw, and he worshiped, and he prayed.

And she said, "Forgive them, Peter, for they know not what they do." And he hated them, and he loved her.

And then she left him.

Close the door, Peter, he told himself. Close the goddamned door and keep it closed.

* * *

Arnie hung up the phone with a shaking hand. Leesha put cool fingers on the back of his neck. "He answered?" she said.

"Yeah." Gentle pressure from her hand brought him

back down to the pillows. He leaned against the headboard. "What the fuck am I going to do?"

"What did he say?"

"Nothing. Nothing."

She handed him his Jack Daniel's, and he drank it down, then handed it back to her. She refilled it from the bottle on the nightstand and handed it back to him.

He took a sip. "What the fuck am I going to do?" he asked again.

"Arnie, honey," she said, then she put her cool fingertips on his hot cheek and turned his face toward her. "Let him go, honey, he's got his own life to live the way he needs to live it."

"He's dying."

"You don't know that."

"He's gone over the edge, Leesha."

"It's his privilege."

"What kind of a parent would think that? Don't you think I owe him all the help I can give him?"

"He doesn't want your help, Arnie. You've got to let him be who he is, and do what he does."

"You're a cold bitch, Leesha."

"I don't think so, Arnie. I think you need some distance."

"Distance! This distance crap. That's all you talk about. Distance and letting go. That's my boy. That's my son. My only son. My only family. I owe him." The dry heat came up his throat again. "I owe myself."

"Time."

"Time! I've given him time. It's June, Leesha. I haven't

seen him since December. Six months. Six months he's been in that apartment with that girl, doing God-knows-what. Six months I've been in limbo, tortured. Six months he doesn't want to talk to me. Six months he's not had a breath of fresh air. Six months he's eaten Twinkies and shit. What do you think is happening to him?"

"When he has enough of it, he'll come out. He'll come around."

"Yeah, if he doesn't die."

"If he doesn't die."

"And what if he does? Then what? Then where am I?"

"Not dead."

"Not dead. Wife dead. Son dead. I might as well be dead."

She snuggled up to him. He lifted his arm to let her snuggle close, then closed her in and ran his hand up and down her soft skin.

"You're a good man, Arnie. This is not your fault."

"Yes it is," he said. "It's all my fault."

"How could it be?"

"If it's not mine, then whose is it?"

JULY

When the knock came on the door, Peter froze, his face immobilized. His breathing came hard, and the cords stood out on his neck.

"It's just the food, Peter," Tess whispered. She walked to the door and said, "Who is it?"

There was a long pause, then a voice said, "Delivery from Fifth Street Deli."

"Just leave it at the door," she said, then listened carefully for the familiar sounds of footsteps walking down the hall, the elevator bell, and the doors closing behind the delivery boy. Instead, she heard what she thought was whispering. She listened closer, put her ear up to the door, but she must have been hearing things, or maybe Peter's paranoia had become contagious. The delivery boy was probably just muttering to himself. She heard him put the box down, then the footsteps. Then the elevator bell, the doors opening, the doors closing.

She slid the chain back, turned the bolt, then opened the door, and it shoved against her, slamming her against the wall.

Peter's father strode in. "Peter? Peter, dammit, boy, come out here." He walked into the bedroom.

Tess pushed the apartment door closed and scrabbled sideways across the kitchen to a dishtowel that lay on the floor. It covered most of her skinny torso.

"Je-sus Christ! Look at you, son. What the hell is going on here?"

Tess cowered. What if he took Peter away?

Then Arnie was standing over her in the kitchen, his round face red, his yellow shirt too bright for her eyes, and then he grabbed her arm and pulled her up and into the bedroom with him. He threw her on the bed next to Peter.

His intrusion was terrible. Tess looked at his face, he had so much flesh on him. He was chubby, pudgy, he was more than that, he was healthy and filled. She looked around the room, at the sheets that had gone dingy and yellow because they'd been too busy to change them—they still had the solid black line down the center—she looked at the food wrappers that had been kicked into the corner of the room, at the papers and drawings and little note things that littered the floor. She smelled the freshness on him; the stale air of the apartment suddenly seemed dangerous. He was horrible, he was damaging, he was ripping giant holes in their lives.

"Don't you eat?" he was saying. Peter was scrunched up into a little ball at the head of the bed, hugging his pillow.

"Talk to me!" His father ripped the sheet off of him, pulled the pillow away from him. "I'm calling an ambulance. The two of you need something. You need something, some kind of help, that's for sure." He reached for the telephone.

"I'll die first," Peter said, his voice soft yet solid.

"I beg your pardon?"

"You heard me," Peter said. He put his pillow down, sat up and reached for Tess. She connected with his strength. Admiration flushed through her. He knew what to do, he instinctively knew how to handle this situation. She pulled strength from him, changed from a quivering little girl into a queen, dropped the dish towel and took her place at the head of the bed. "Leave us alone. We have a right to be left alone."

Peter's father looked from face to face. "Listen, son. You've got a lovely girl here. She should have a better life. Go outside. Get some sun. Eat a pizza. Eat a salad. Get a job, get married, have a few kids—"

Have a few kids! Rage flushed through Tess.

"Enough! Get out. Get out!"

"You're dying, Peter, can't you see that? Look at you."

Peter looked at his father, then reached for his journal and began to draw.

"Peter." No response. "Peter!"

Tess saw what he was drawing and interpreted it for him. "If Peter had a gun, he'd kill you," she said.

"You're the one who needs help here, young lady. I won't let you destroy my son. I'll be back. I'll be back." He left the room, and Tess watched him step over the box of groceries at the doorway. "Doughnuts. Ice cream. Hi-Hos. Chocolate. Marshmallows. Popcorn. Beer! No wonder!" He kicked the door. "No wonder!" He pointed a finger at her. "I'll be back." And then he stomped off. Tess heard the elevator bell, the door open, and then close. She got off the bed, pulled in the box of groceries, and then closed and locked the door. She brought the marshmallows and a six-pack of Heineken back to the bed, and ripped open the bag.

The two of them watched each other in silence and ate every marshmallow.

"What'll we do, Peter?" Tess asked.

Peter stared at her. Tess loved Peter, but his ways had begun to annoy her. This stare, for example, had become his response to anything she asked. It was short of accusatory, but not by much. Everything seemed to be her fault, and she was a little tired of either apologizing or explaining all the time.

"Stop it, Peter, I'm tired of you staring at me like that all the time. You never say what's on your mind, you expect me to just somehow know what you're thinking."

Peter looked down at his hands. Then he said, "If you were one with me, you would know what I think."

"I try, but I'm not perfect yet."

"You try to be separate."

"No, I don't."

"You let him in."

There she was again, off balance. "Let him in? He forced his way in. He pushed the door open, Peter, I hit the wall." She looked at him, but he wouldn't meet her gaze. "He hurt me."

"You let him in."

"I didn't."

"You knew he was out there."

"I did not."

"You did, because you called him. You called him. You called him in the middle of the night when I was asleep. I saw the phone cord."

"What?" Tess was beside herself.

"I know all about it. Deception. Lies." Peter's eyes burned into her.

"You're wrong," she said softly.

"Wrong?"

"I'm sorry, Peter, you are."

"I could kill you," he said with eerie gentleness.

Desperate for his love and affection, Tess began to tremble. How could he accuse her? She loved him, she devoted her existence to him. She wanted to support him, help him, he was her entire life!

But she couldn't help him, she couldn't finish their important work if she were threatened. If they didn't work together, they couldn't get the job done.

And the gospel was the most important thing in the world. More important than anything else. He could kill her and that would be all right. Abandoning the project would not be all right.

"Draw, Peter," she said. "Work it out. Tell your story."

"I could kill you so easy," he said, that same look in his eyes.

"If you killed me, then we wouldn't be able to write the gospel. You should protect me, just like I'm trying to protect you. This is our work, Peter. Our lifetime work."

"My work," he said. He sat up, then got up on his knees. He towered over her, and she felt her heart pound in fear. He could actually kill me, she realized with a horrible flash of insight, and nobody would miss me. She knew what would stop him, and in fear, she acted.

"I'd haunt you," she said.

It worked. His face softened and he rested back on his heels.

Power surged through her. "I'd come back screaming and hissing at you at all hours. You'd never be able to finish your work, because I'd poke and prod and never let you concentrate. And then I really would call your father, and I'd haunt him until he took you to a place where they kept loonies."

Peter looked like he was going to cry. Tess sat up in satisfaction, although it was short-lived. She hated scaring him. He was her partner, she had no right to control him with his own fears like that. But, she reasoned, he controlled her with threats of killing her, didn't he?

"Draw, Peter," she said softly. "Draw out the experience. Put down what it means to you." He turned on his side, away from her, but she saw the glint of a tear in the corner of his eye. Further damage, she thought. I've done further damage to us. But since it's for the good of the Word, everything will turn out okay, over time. Over eternity.

She picked up her journal and began to write. Eventually, Peter reached for his, and he began to draw, sketch really, with little light strokes. Tess watched him and wrote about how Peter's father had burst in upon them, and what that had done to Peter, and how she had resolved the situation, although it was still possible that she'd be sacrificed for his work. Then she wrote about luck and curses and hauntings, and wondered if she really could come back and haunt someone.

She would haunt Charles, she thought, and that name floated up through the depths of her memory as if it had been trapped within a sea chest. She'd forgotten about Charles; hadn't thought of him for months.

She thought of herself in his house, as his wife, and she couldn't imagine it. She couldn't even bring his face into focus in her memory. She could only remember the pain and the pain and then the panic of having to go out and work for a living, or else find her way among a whole new set of people, develop all new friends, form a new society after Charles closed the door on all that had been familiar for all those years.

She threw her journal down and snuggled up to Peter's back, wrapped her arms around him, her legs around him.

"Fwiggle gort," she said, and he turned to her and held her and they both cried.

* * *

Peter lay on his stomach, wishing he could sleep as easily as Tess. He punched his pillow onto the floor, then lay with his cheek to the sheet and both arms down at his sides, his toes off the foot of the bed.

For a moment, he was home, lying on the cold concrete

of his father's garage, smelling the oil, the footprints, the dog. He was lying there for no particular reason, still wearing his tennis whites. He'd come back from a good match, one that he'd won, and while walking through the garage, just decided to lie down on the floor and feel and smell and taste. He licked the concrete. The floor tried to suck all the moisture out of his tongue. His tongue kind of stuck to it.

Then he heard the garage door open, and he knew if he scrambled up, then they would think he'd been doing something wrong, so he just continued to lie there, tensed, all the pleasure of his time alone with the garage floor gone.

"Petie? Honey?"

It was his mother, and she clacked over in her high heels, having been to the doctor again, silk scarf brushing the back of his head as she bent down to him. She was sick, Peter knew. She was sick, very, very sick, and although she sometimes smelled a little sick, she didn't look sick, she didn't act sick, and that was why it was so hard for him to accept that she was going to die.

"Pete?"

He felt her cool hand on his ear, then the back of his neck as she smoothed her cool fingers around him. He wanted to turn over, look into her blue eyes and grab her, hold her, sob into her breast, and then ask her to lie on the floor and taste the concrete with him. Had she ever tasted concrete? Had she ever put her forehead, hot and sweaty from a victory match, on the dirty, gritty garage floor? Would she die without that experience?

But he did nothing. He merely said, "Hmm?"

"Are you all right?

"Um-hmm."

"How did you do?"

"I won," he said, and the floor muffled his words.

"Good for you, Petie. Good for you. I'm so proud of you."

Peter heard the words catch in her throat, and he knew that she just remembered that she'd never live to see him at Wimbledon. God damn!

Then she touched his head again, stood up, and without another word, without asking him why he was lying face down on the garage floor, she clacked her heels to the door, opened it, and entered the kitchen.

Peter clenched his fists. Come back here! Talk to me! Be with me! Mommy! Mommy! All those things he should have said, should have done.

The garage floor lost its attraction. He stood up, chilled from the damp cold of it, and went to his room.

The next morning, his mother slept in. He went to practice, then to class, and she was still in bed when he came home. He read, watched TV, fiddled around, and then started dinner. He was feeling increasingly antsy. At five o'clock, he went in to see if she needed anything, and there she was, peaceful and cold. He left her there. At five-thirty, his father came home from work. The two of them sat silently, self-consciously, at the kitchen table, waiting for the police, the ambulance, the coroner. The house was filled with a silence like he'd never known before. He wondered if that's what they meant when they said "silent as death." There was no other silence like it.

Drug overdose, the coroner said. Self-administered.

She couldn't live with the knowledge that she would die. She couldn't accept the inevitable. Peter knew that he would never live to know many things, but he knew that he was the reason for his mother's suicide.

She would never live to see him at Wimbledon, and she could not live with that knowledge.

If he'd not had such aspirations, maybe she would still be here.

Peter clenched fists of sheet and tensed his muscles. He wanted to squeeze, to hurt, to bite, to tear. Instead, he took a deep breath and relaxed. Another deep breath, relax. Another, relaaaax. His grip loosened and he tucked his arms underneath him. But he couldn't erase the memory of his mother's cold, dead face.

* * *

Arnie paced back and forth in his bedroom. "I can't believe I left them there. Now I have to figure out how to get back in there again. I'll need a court order or something. I can't believe I did it. I should have grabbed Peter right out of there and taken him to a hospital. God!"

"There'll come a time, Arnie, when you'll have to stop this or die yourself."

Arnie stopped pacing and sat on the bed. "You didn't see them, Leesha."

"No, I didn't. But I see that they don't want you in their lives."

"They are fucking skeletons. And they were right out of their heads. They'll die. They are dying."

"So are we all."

"They're so young. They've got so much ahead of them."

"You don't know that."

That stopped him. Most of what Leesha said made sense, most of what Leesha said he could either accept or argue with. But that—that stopped him. "What do you mean?"

"I mean when Fran's time was up, you didn't agree with that, either."

"You think Peter's time is up?"

"I think that's not for you to decide. That's between him and his god."

"I'm his father, for Chrissake."

"Yes. His father. That little boy was a gift to you, and you were to tend it, nourish it, and help it along its way until it flew the nest. And what happens after that is not for you to decide."

Arnie hung his head. Leesha reached over and scratched his scalp with her fingernails. It felt great.

"A parent's job description changes when the kid leaves, Arnie, and hardly anybody knows that. That's why there are so many mother-in-law problems and why there are so many jokes about parents coming to visit. When your kids are grown up, your job as a parent is finished. Your role changes. You're to love them and support them in their positive decisions, just like you would any good friend."

"There is nothing positive there."

"Then there's nothing to support except Peter's right to be Peter and make his own decisions. But you can't change him and you can't change those decisions. You can't run Peter's life like you used to. You changed his diapers. Then you coached him. For twenty-four hours every day, his life was in your hands. Well, no more. And as soon as you come to terms with that, perhaps he'll come out of that apartment."

Anger flushed through Arnie. Anger that came from the fear that it was his fault. "Don't you blame me for...."

"Shhh," she said, and then kissed his neck.

In spite of himself, his body began to respond to her. He was getting used to having Leesha around. She was good for him. Real good.

"Look what I found," she whispered. "Now here's something positive."

He lay back and let Leesha work her particular brand of magic on him. "Leesha," he said.

"Hmm?"

"How do you know these things, I mean about a parent's job description changing?"

"School of hard knocks, Arnie."

"You're pretty smart. And you've got such a nice ass."

She matched her skin to his and slid up his side, then kissed him on the side of the neck. He wrapped his arms around her. "I don't know how smart," she whispered, and let her hand fall away.

"What?"

"I'm falling in love with you, Arnie, and I don't think that's a very good idea."

"You are?" The news astonished him.

"See? If it was a smart thing, you wouldn't be so surprised. You'd have seen it coming. In a perfect world, you would be falling in love with me, as well."

Arnie felt the heat evaporate from his loins. He didn't know what to think.

Peter. Fran. Leesha. Life was certainly filled with burdens.

A little headache sprouted right between his eyes. He rolled over on his side away from her and cradled his head in his arms.

She snuggled up against his back, doodling lightly on his shoulder blade with her fingernail. "Not smart at all," she whispered.

AUGUST

Tess awakened feeling obstinate and angry. She crossed her arms over her chest. This room is ugly, she thought, and it stinks.

She looked at Peter, who snored softly beside her. His teeth looked furred, his breath smelled like rotten snails, his fingernails were dirty.

"Peter, get up. Get up! You stink. Go shower." She began pulling the pillowcases off the pillows and pulling on the bottom sheet, the sheet that still had the dark line down the middle. That sheet had sort of become a symbol to them, and they'd been reluctant to change it. It was a memory of a horrible time, but an important time—a growing time. Those times of pain and hurt were the most important. But enough was enough.

Peter groaned and opened his eyes. They narrowed as they watched her scurry around the bedroom, kicking food containers into the big pile in the corner. "C'mon. Get up. Take a shower. Let's get the dishes done and change these scuzzy sheets. C'mon!"

Peter slowly sat up, then swung his legs over the bed. He

took a deep breath and began to cough. He'd started coughing barely a week ago, and the congestion had progressed rapidly. He coughed and coughed without control, with barely a breath, and when he was finished, perspiration dotted his forehead.

"Go," Tess said. "The steam will do your lungs good."

Peter looked at her with that narrow expression, and then reached into the bottom drawer of the nightstand, removed the telephone and took it to the bathroom with him.

"Asshole," she said, and finished ripping the sheets from the bed. She laid the sheets on the floor, kicked all the trash from the corner into them, then tied the corners together into a bundle. Peter can take this to the trash chute, she thought. There's no saving those sheets. She hauled it to the kitchen and set it next to the door. Then she had to rest. The exertion was almost too much. The kitchen was a mess, but it would have to wait until another day.

She heard the toilet, and then the shower. She got clean sheets from the dryer where they'd lain wrinkling for months and threw them in a pile on the bed. She lay on top of them for a while, catching her breath, and then she smelled herself, smelled her stickiness, her musk, and suddenly couldn't wait for Peter to finish in the shower.

She opened the bathroom door. The blast of hot steam felt great. She smelled toothpaste and soap, and it smelled wonderful. She felt as if she were coming out of a long, horribly distorted dream.

She whipped the shower curtain aside, and there was

Peter, leaning against the shower wall, soaped up penis in hand, stroking slowly.

Fury flushed through Tess. "What are you doing?"

He slowly opened his eyes and looked at her.

She began to cry. "It's not right, you know. It's not right. You kidnap me, you rape me, you ignore me, you abuse me. And then you won't even make love to me anymore. You never make love to me anymore! Never!"

Peter continued to look at her, but he gave no indication that he heard her. He was absorbed in his own soapy activity.

"I hate you for this," she said.

He just looked at her.

"Hate you! Hate you!" She hit him in the arm, then hit him in the chest. "I hate you!"

Peter put up his hand to defend himself, and Tess grabbed it. She pulled him out of the tub, felt him slip and slide behind her as she hauled him out of the bathroom and into the bedroom. She threw him down on the pile of clean sheets and jumped on top of him.

His erection had disappeared, and Peter looked at her with fear in his face.

"Bring it back. Bring it back!" She slapped him on the chest with one hand and grabbed his penis with her other one. "It's mine, goddamn it, Peter, and don't you forget it. It's mine, and I want it. Now. Now. Give it to me now!" She raised her hand to slap him again, and he caught her hand, rolled her over and began to kiss her.

It felt so good, it felt so wonderful, it had been so long

since he'd kissed her, a fresh toothpaste kiss. Oh God, she needed him. She hugged him and kissed him back, melting under the heat of him.

She felt his erection against her belly, and felt her readiness for him. I'll make love to him, she thought. This is my treat. She moved against him, kissing him deeply, fiercely. Then she rolled him over onto his back again, straddled him, then lowered herself slowly, ever so slowly, onto him. Oh God, it was wonderful.

She closed her eyes and moved slowly, moved to the internal rhythm that propelled the universe.

Then she felt him buck, and his penis withered.

She opened her eyes and looked at him. He squinted back at her. "You could've waited," she said.

"I could've," he said.

Before she realized what she was doing, Tess, still filled with a rising tide of passion, clenched her fist and smashed it into his mouth.

He threw her off as he rolled onto the floor. Her knuckles bled; she'd gashed them open on his teeth.

Peter was whining and moaning on the floor, and when she looked over the side of the bed, she saw his mouth was filled with blood, too. It ran out between his fingers. His eyes were haunted; they looked at her with hurt and pain and confusion.

She glared back at him, and only after he scrambled to his feet and left the bedroom, did she hold her damaged hand and bounce up and down with the pain.

When he returned from the bathroom, his cut lips swelling and bruised, she was making the bed. He seemed subdued. He helped her.

"Take out the trash," she said, and he obeyed.

She got into the fresh bed and turned on her side, away from him.

When he came back, he had popcorn, but she wasn't hungry. "Write, Tessa," he said, but she ignored him, even though she knew he was right.

"Die," she said.

Peter ate popcorn through swollen lips and was silent.

Later, when hunger pangs overcame her solitude, she slid to the bottom of the bed and reached for the old wooden popcorn bowl. There were only unpopped kernels left. She picked one out and sucked on it.

"Is there any food?" she asked Peter. She knew the answer. He shook his head.

She got up, went to the bathroom and picked up the telephone from the back of the toilet. She brought it back to the bedroom, handed it to him and said, "Order."

Peter took the phone, staring at her with that uncomfortable squinty way he had. He plugged it in and pushed the numbers for the deli. He ordered five different kinds of cookies and a case of beer.

Good. He hung up the phone, never once taking his eyes from her. Well, she could stand that. She could stare him down if she had to. He wasn't going to abuse her any longer. They were committed to each other and he had to learn that meant he was to respect her wishes, respect her body, respect her in every way. The way she respected him.

The phone rang.

They both jumped at the intrusion. They had been so intent on each other's eyes, small movements the other made to indicate whether or not they would break eye contact, and then the phone rang and they both looked at it, and neither one knew which looked away first.

It rang again.

Peter jerked on the cord and it came out. The phone was permanently silenced. The little plastic plug was still in the wall.

They were cut off. Tess knew the meaning of this. This was it. This was the ultimate. Once the cookies and beer arrived, they were without a way to call for more, they were without a way to call for help.

That's silly, she thought. I can tell the man when he delivers the food to bring us something else. I can always go to a neighbor's if we need help.

But she wouldn't, she knew she wouldn't. That was part of it. That was what Peter had done. He'd dared her, and she knew she would not back down first.

When the food came, Tess took a package of macaroons and a package of M&Ms. Peter took the chocolate chips and the cake wafers. They split the Oreos. They split up the beer, too, each stashing bottles in the respective bottom drawers of each nightstand. Tess had to reshuffle her pile of notebooks, but eventually it all fit.

I'm going to have to find a place to pee, Tess thought, because he'll rob me if I leave him with my food.

Or I'll take it with me when I go.

Thus settled, she slept.

They awoke to a banging on the front door, and someone saying, "Police! Open up!"

Tess reached for Peter, but he wasn't there. She sat up and rubbed her eyes, and then she saw him, walking toward the door. He made it to the door before a coughing spasm took him to his knees.

"Peter, this is your father." The voice came through loud and clear, all the way to the bedroom. Tess jumped out of bed, steadied herself until the blackness left her vision, and then went to Peter and put her arm around him.

He looked at her with haunted eyes. The look in his eyes shocked her, and when he shrugged her off, she left him alone.

"Peter, I've come back with the police. You won't answer the door, boy, you won't answer the phone, so I've got the police here to force their way in."

"Peter, this is Detective Anderson. Open this door, please."

Peter made his way to the door on hands and knees. He put his cheek against it, and Tess knew he was going to let them in. He put his hand against it, next to his cheek. Out of the bedroom, away from his element, his thin body looked dangerously sick.

"Daddy?" he said in a weak voice.

"Peter!"

"Daddy, go away."

"No, Peter, open up. Come on, now."

"I don't want you here, please, Dad, if you love me, you'll leave me alone."

Tess was surprised, sort of. She hadn't expected this, yet it was Peter who had issued the challenge to her, and if he'd let his father and the police in now, that would be an admission of defeat. A breach of their agreement.

And yet, maybe someone ought to see to Peter's cough. It had become pretty bad.

There was talk on the other side of the door. Tess heard the elevator bell.

"Peter?"

"Hmm?"

It sounded like Peter's father was sitting on the floor on the other side of the door. "Peter, I sent the police away, so you can open the door and it will only be me."

Tess knew that the police wouldn't open the door against Peter's wishes. It was a strong arm tactic, and it hadn't worked. Good for Peter. She thought about his stash of cookies, and how she could just go in and take two chocolate chip ones and Peter would never know it. She looked back at the empty bedroom. Instead, she stayed to listen and watch.

"How long have you had that cough, boy?"

"Don't know." Peter leaned his forehead against the door.

"Doesn't sound good. Have you seen anybody about it? No, I suppose not. Are you taking anything?"

Silence.

"Peter, are you still there?" There was panic in his voice.

"Yes."

"Good, good. Listen, this is good, us having a little talk like this. I like it. Do you like it?"

"No."

"Well, then I appreciate it all the more. How's your lady friend there? She's right pretty, Peter. The two of you getting along all right?"

Peter turned and looked at Tess, his lips swollen, his top one split with a black line of dried blood and scab down the middle of it. He didn't answer.

"You have food to eat, Peter? Peter?"

"Go away, Dad," he said, and stood up.

"Peter? Peter? I'll come back tomorrow, Peter, maybe we can talk again, okay? Okay?"

Tess could hear Arnie touch the outside of the door as if it were his son. His hands moved gently on its surface. "I love you, boy," he said.

Peter walked past her into the bedroom and lay on the bed. When she came in, he looked at her, then opened the bottom drawer and checked his food. Tess pretended not to notice. She picked up her journal and began to write.

* * *

At his mother's funeral, Peter's father cried throughout the whole ceremony. Peter wished he could get up and move to sit behind him, or one seat over from him or something, because listening to his father cry was the worst thing he could imagine. It was even worse than finding his mother dead. The little tiny sounds of sniffing and swallowing and wiping and fidgeting that his father made reamed holes in Peter's insides. He didn't want to see it, hear it, feel it, know about it. It embarrassed him.

He couldn't concentrate on what was said at the service, and when it was over, he realized he didn't remember a single thing that was said. And it was all his dad's fault.

Later, his father moaned and turned away during the middle of the graveside ceremony, and Peter wanted to punch him. And then, as the mourners filed past, shaking hands and kissing cheeks, Peter's father hugged him too tightly and said, "You're all I've got now, son. We'll get through this together."

Peter didn't want to be all his father had. He didn't want to get through anything together with him. He wanted his father to stand up and act like a man, to be a man, to find within himself the capacity of many things, not just looking over the shoulder of his son.

Peter wanted to grab him by the lapels, right there at his mother's grave and say, "Get hold of yourself, Dad. Find a new interest. Find a new life. I'm moving on, and I can't carry you." But that wasn't appropriate—it wasn't the right time or place. He marked those words in his memory, though, because the time would come when he would say them. Right then, he just wanted to get to the tennis courts.

He went home, took off his suit and went to practice while his dad got drunk with the neighbors.

I don't know what you expect of me, Dad, he thought.

I know you want me to be everything for you, but you are nothing for me. Nothing! Nothing but a pain in the ass.

Peter picked up his journal and began to draw. He drew long, luminescent teardrops, with his father trapped inside each one.

* * *

"I've got a surprise, Arnie." Leesha handed him a Jack Daniel's, sipped her own and grinned at his questioning look. "Guess."

"Leesha. C'mon. Just tell me."

She reached behind the pillow on the couch and brought out two airline tickets. "Banff," she said. "One week. Out of the heat, into the cool mountains. The Canadian Rockies." She saw the look on his face, came over and sat by him. Then she took his hands in hers and looked earnestly into his face. "Lake Louise," she said. "Pine trees. Beautiful. Beautiful. Have you ever been there?"

Arnie hung his head. Shook it no.

"We leave on Sunday."

"Leesha...." He sighed.

"We're going, Arnie. I love you and I need to take you out of here for a while. One week."

"I can't."

"You can. You must. You will."

"He's talking to me, Leesha, he's finally talking to me."

"He'll talk to you when we get back."

"No. Every day. Every day I go over there and sit on the floor in front of his door, and he sits on the floor on his side of the door, and we touch, we touch through the door, you don't understand."

"I do understand, Arnie. I understand that you've lost weight, that you're starting to lose interest in sex. You don't eat right, you don't sleep well. I've just found you, honey, I can't lose you the way I lost Mickey."

"You're not losing me, Leesha."

"Yes, I am. So." She gently slapped the tickets on his knee. "This is the deal. We go away together for a few days or I'm out of your life."

Arnie looked at her again with amazement. "You can't be serious."

"Totally serious."

"Leesha…" He looked at her, her perky face, her carefully done hair, her big blue eyes that so rarely looked this solemn.

He would miss her. He would genuinely miss her. "Just another month or two."

"I've given you six months, Arnie. You're obsessed. I need to know that you can live some kind of a balanced life. I need to know that I matter to you at all. I need to see you laugh and have some fun. I need to go away with you for a while, Arnie. Now. So if you value my presence at all in your life, you will go with me. If not, then you'll have to sit by Peter's door for your entertainment and companionship."

Arnie felt squeezed. Why was everybody so damned demanding? He put his arm around her and brought her to him. She fit against him perfectly.

"He's sick, Leesha. I can't leave my son when he's so sick."

"You have to have your own life, Arnie. Peter is sick, that's true. He has the right to refuse treatment for his sickness."

"He's not competent to make that decision."

"He is. He's an adult."

"He's my son."

"I know, Arnie. And I know this is killing you. That's why I want to take you away for a week."

"You don't understand."

"I understand that I love you. I understand that you have to have your own life. You have to live for you, Arnie, not for some ungrateful kid who wants to die a slow death. Don't let him torture you to death, too. Please. Please."

He lifted his hand, opened his mouth, but there was no gesture to be made, no words to be said.

"We leave Sunday," she said, and an alternate world presented itself to Arnie. A world where he could just pick up and go to Canada for a week, where he could leave everything. He'd never been able to do that before. First there was school, and parents, and then there was the Navy. He thought he would find freedom in the Navy, but there was none. There was only responsibility and more responsibility. And right out of the Navy, he met Fran, and then there was night school, and the baby, and then the coaching, that never let up, not for a moment, then Fran's illness, and then Peter's accident, and now Peter's illness....

Would he ever be free?

It was up to him. He could take off now. He could leave on Sunday, go with Leesha. They could screw in the elevator if they wanted, they could do it in the Jacuzzi. He could just lock the door and they could jump on that plane, and never give another thought to anything. He had no pets, he had no job, he had plenty of money for his simple tastes, he could just go.

It was tempting, so very tempting.

But that was not Arnie's life. Arnie's life was not filled with impetuous, spontaneous improvisations. Some people had that kind of life, but not Arnie. Leesha needed to find someone who could have the same type of fun that she had. He had to see to his responsibilities, and Peter was still his responsibility, no matter what anybody else said or thought or how they tried to convince him otherwise.

No, Arnie couldn't go to Canada with Leesha. Not now, probably not ever. But for a moment, entertaining the idea was very nice.

"I can't go," he said, and the knife that cut her loose also sliced him deeper than he thought it would.

"I'm so sorry," she whispered, then struggled free from him, and without a backward glance, downed her drink, picked up her purse and left.

SEPTEMBER

Tess opened her eyes and thought that the only difference between being awake and being asleep is that when you're asleep, somebody else tells you stories. The story she'd just been dreaming had to do with her best friend in grade school, Debbie Nessman. Tess and Ness. They were the hopscotch champions. Tess had her lucky necklace she'd throw into the square, and Debbie had an ankle chain. They were good at jumping rope, too, both could jump Double Dutch better than anybody else. At recess, they would go out to the monkey bars and stand around and talk about boys and parents and hairstyles, speculate about sex and gossip about who in their class was "ig'nrant." They felt superior. They were superior. Debbie moved away just before seventh grade. Tess never had a friend that good again.

Tess stared at the ceiling and remembered Debbie Nessman. Where was Debbie now?

Peter moved beside her. She looked at him. His drawing was in his lap, the pencil in his hand. He stared at the wall.

"Did you know Debbie?"she asked, confused, for a moment, by the way time can fold in upon itself.

166

Peter just looked at her.

No, Tess thought. Of course not. Debbie wouldn't like Peter very much. She rolled over and opened the nightstand drawer. Two macaroons and a beer. Good. She closed the drawer again. They were there in case she needed them. Peter hadn't robbed her yet. His food was long gone, and she hadn't eaten since—well, in a while.

She pulled the current journal out from under her pillow and began to write. Writing was the most important thing left. It was the only thing.

Tess's fingers wouldn't hold the pen. They had no strength. She shook her hand, she slapped it against the bed. She held the hand in her fist.

"Itch," Peter said.

Tess ignored him. Concentrating was hard enough without him trying to scratch his itches on her. She slipped off the bed and walked over to the pile of sheets in the corner. She squatted and peed, then came back to the bed and tried the pen again. She found a little more muscle control. "Nearing breakthrough," she wrote. And that's all she could manage. She wanted to write how free she felt without food. She wanted to say how the human race and all its ills were because of its addiction to food, when food wasn't even necessary to life. It wasn't even necessary! Food was the bane of human existence. It kept people tied to the ground, it kept them heavy and sedated. Without food, the spirit roamed free.

"Itch," Peter said.

Tess looked over at him. He didn't itch; his penis wasn't even hard.

Tess looked down at her journal. She wished she had the strength to write those things about food. She wished she hadn't written only the story of Peter, because there were so many other things she'd thought of, so many important things that she hadn't written down.

As it was, in her last notebook she'd had to write two lines in every ruled space, in the margins and on both covers as well. This book was almost filled to the brim with the story of Peter and the documentation of his life, his faith, his self-denial and his holiness. If she had only the strength and the materials to write one thing, it was best she wrote what was most important.

The tapping started again on the door. Peter's father came every day. When Peter didn't open the door, his father would sit on the floor and try to talk to him. Sometimes he cried. If Peter wouldn't talk, his father would just tap. Tap tap tap. For an hour.

"Peter? It's your dad."

Peter's pupils dilated slightly. He turned to Tess and said, "Sacrifice."

Strength surged into Tess and she found her pen. She needed more writing space. She picked at the cardboard backing on her notebook and began to separate the pieces into separate sheets. She'd have two completely clean pages in which to continue The Word. This was so important. This was so exciting.

Peter slowly stood up, leaning against the wall. A coughing spasm overtook him, and by the time he was finished, his face was pale and this throat was cherry red. He wiped his hand over his face, then limped into the kitchen, took a paring knife from the drawer and began to unlock the door. Tess sat on her heels and watched, intently. She didn't want to miss a thing. Sacrifice! Sacrifice! Of course! There was a symmetry to it, something so perfect, so basic, and yet, something didn't quite add up.

Peter opened the door.

Peter's father stood there, looking smaller than he had before. He was paler, and there were deep lines etched into the flesh of his face.

"Peter...."

Peter stood back, holding the door open. Tess saw him look at her, and she sat, sniffing the air, waiting, tense, alert.

Peter's father walked into the kitchen, wary. Peter closed the door, then with a roundhouse swing, swiped at his father's neck with the knife.

His father grabbed his wrist as if Peter were a child, and took the knife from him. "What is this, son?"

Peter howled. He wailed like a sick animal. All the years of pain and suffering and hatred and disappointment boiled up and out of him in a pitiful cry of defeat that was too much for Tess to bear. How dare this ugly, fleshy thing, this sacrifice thing defeat her king? She mustered her energy, scampered off the bed and ran into the kitchen. Peter's father turned toward her and she plunged her pen deeply into the hollow of his throat.

His big eyes bulged wide with surprise. He dropped the knife. Blood seeped out around the wound. He couldn't move his head. He didn't seem to be able to breathe right.

Peter picked up the knife. His father sank to his knees, hands groping for the blue shaft that protruded from just below his Adam's apple.

Peter put the knife point to his father's neck and pressed. The skin stretched, then parted. His father winced. Peter dropped the knife. His father writhed and choked on the floor.

And then Arnie pulled the pen out.

Blood gushed onto the floor.

Tess looked wildly around her for a way to end this terrible, terrible scene. She opened a cabinet. There was an unopened quart of mayonnaise. She took it from the shelf and threw it down on Arnie's head as hard as she could. The jar broke, splattering all three of them with greasy white globs mixed with shards, and Peter's father thumped unconscious on the kitchen floor.

Liquid blood breaths burbled out of his lips.

Peter looked at Tess. He began to cough, a long, terrible wheezing spell. When he was finished, he was pale and trembling. He reached over and pinched his father's nose and his lips together. Arnie stopped breathing. His chest continued to move. Blood swished out of the hole in his throat as shallow breaths gurgled through into his lungs.

"Cut him," Tess said.

"Why doesn't he die?"

"He won't die just because you want him to. You have to do it."

Peter took the knife again. He pinched the area of the neck where he'd tried to cut before. The skin was so thin. "Just saw on him?"

Tess cringed. "Don't know, Peter. Do something!"

Peter looked at the door. "In the bedroom," he said.

"No. The bedroom is ours."

Peter looked like he was going to cry.

"Knife in the heart," Tess said.

Peter rocked back on his heels. He wiped at his face and smeared bloodied mayonnaise on his forehead.

His father's eyelids fluttered.

"Do something, Peter."

"Daddy?"

Tess got the cleaver from the drawer. It was incredibly heavy. She pushed Peter away, squatted in front of the old man's face, turned his head the other way, and with both hands, brought the heavy cleaver down through his neck.

It stuck solidly in the linoleum.

Blood pumped. Eyelids fluttered, then opened. Peter's father locked eyes with his son, his fingers moved, and then as if he were falling asleep, they closed again. The pool of blood grew, the gurgling continued. His feet twitched.

They squatted next to him until he was dead.

It took a long time.

Peter lay across his father's body. "He loved me," he said.

Tess lay next to Peter, caressing his shoulders, picking stray bits of mayonnaise jar from his hair and beard. "He still does," she said.

Peter lay his head on his father's chest and fell asleep. Tess watched him for a few moments— the word "trinity" kept floating through her mind—and then she, too, was sleep in the escaping warmth.

When she woke up, Peter was staring at her.

"You killed him," he said.

"Sacrifice," she said, and suddenly understood what was missing when Peter wanted to kill him. A sacrifice was always to something. This was her sacrifice to Peter. "My sacrifice to you, my God," she said.

Peter threw a glob of jellied blood at her. It hit her thigh and spattered into chunks, like black jello.

She laughed, scooped some up and threw it back at him.

They leaned together and smeared blood on each other, and Tess noticed that Peter had a giant erection, his first in a long time. She scooted toward him, opened herself, and they rutted wildly alongside the corpse. But there was no emotion in it. They lost interest after a few moments, and disengaged.

"Shower together?"

'No," he said. He picked up another clump of blood and drew lines on her chest and cheeks.

Tess felt an overwhelming love for him. She wished that somehow, things could have been different for them.

And then she remembered The Word.

She took Peter's hand, helped him up and led him back

to the bedroom. When she filled her last two pages, she could write on the sheets. As it turned out, there was a good reason they only had white ones.

* * *

Peter smeared the mayonnaised blood around his belly and thighs and remembered the last time there had been blood all over him. His blood. He was jaywalking across the street, tennis racquet in hand, headed for lunch with his dad, when a car careened around the corner. Peter, filled with victory from the match, was feeling invincible, and though the car came right toward him, he felt confident that the driver would see him and swerve.

He didn't.

He heard his hip shatter when the grille hit him. His knee popped like a rifle. He looked up—time shifted into slow motion—and noticed how gray the sky had turned.

And then he was in the hospital, never really waking, never really sleeping, just pain and relief. Pain and relief. And then pain, relief and Dad. And eventually, nurses, meals, sores on heels and elbows from the starched sheets.

"You'll be fine, boy, just fine," his father said to him every day, then the casts came off and they took him in a wheelchair to try to walk in the physical therapy room, but his legs wouldn't cooperate.

He would never play tennis again.

He lay in the hospital for another month, staring at the ceiling, thinking nothing.

No, that wasn't quite true. He was thinking of all the

hopes and dreams he'd never realize, because of being in the wrong place at the wrong time.

No, that wasn't quite true, either. He had never been quite good enough, and he was already getting too old. The big players, the stars, were already at the top by the time they were nineteen, and he was just beginning the circuit at twenty-two.

But it was easier to talk about the drunk in the Chevy. It was easier to blame the martinis and the poor sot who had no control over his steering wheel.

But he could never say any of this to his father. He burned with forgiveness for that driver, that poor man damned to eternal guilt and a lifetime of court-imposed poverty. He ached to say out loud to himself, to his father, to his attorney, to his nurses, that he wasn't cutting the mustard anyway, and he was grateful, grateful to that man for ending his long term pain by giving him this terrible, fiery, short term pain and perhaps an excuse for a lifetime of mediocrity.

Every day, his father tapped on his door and came in, unbidden, to sit down and talk about his future. A wife, some kids, a good white-collar job...maybe back to school... maybe coaching...maybe announcing for NBC Sports....

But Peter didn't want any of that. He just wanted to be left alone.

Finally, at long last, his father was leaving him alone.

The ache was overwhelmingly deep and hollow.

OCTOBER

Every day, Tess waited for Peter's father to start tapping on the door. Every day she was surprised to remember that he was moldering in the kitchen instead. Smelling terrible.

They'd covered him with all the extra sheets, towels and even the cushions from the living room couch, and that helped, but she could still smell him when she thought about it. Mostly she didn't notice any more. She was too busy.

Tess always thought—whenever she chanced to think about it—that dying was just life seeping away. Death was the absence of life. When life no longer wanted to be on this planet, it just left, flitting away toward a more noble existence in the night. But that wasn't true, that wasn't true at all.

Tess was dying, she knew it, and it was damned hard work. Death was a very active participant, and it was taking all her concentration.

First, and probably foremost, were the physical sensations. Her skin was drawing up, as if little things were sucking on it all the time, all over her. She could ignore it most of the time, but whenever her concentration strayed, it strayed to the crawling of her skin. She always looked to see if she could catch it in the act, but nothing ever looked different.

And her eyes kept getting heavier. Not the lids, although they, too, seemed thicker, but the eyeballs themselves seemed like heavy lead balls. If she exerted herself too much, then lay back on the bed, she had to lie down slowly, because she was afraid her eyeballs would fall right through the mushy flesh behind them and crack her fragile skull.

And she twitched. Ceaselessly. A toe, an eyebrow, thigh, shoulder, something was always involuntarily jerking. The room seemed dim, and she thought perhaps her sight was failing, but she didn't have time to worry about that. Sometimes she got terrible cramps in her legs, in the arches of her feet, in her toes, and just below her shoulder blades. But while the cramps were severe in intensity, they didn't last long. She didn't have enough energy to cramp. She felt cold all the time, not physically shivering, but detached, as if there were nothing meaningful left.

She filled the last bit of white space she could imagine, pronounced the Gospel finished, and laid her pen down at the side of the bed. Sometimes she looked over the side, where she could see all her papers, journals and the like strewn about, pages sticking out from underneath the mattress where she'd hidden them from Peter, and she hoped desperately that they would be published. She worried ceaselessly about the things she meant to say that she wasn't sure she had said. That was her remaining passion: that The Word, in its entirety, get out to the people.

The only thing that bothered her about the writings was

that there wasn't a conclusion. She never took the facts, the evidence, the meanings and values, and drew them up into a denouement. That would have to be left to the reader, she decided. In fact, the reader's conclusion might turn out to be the most important part of all.

She looked at her papers, but she hardly ever looked at Peter. He was no longer a part of her. It was as if they were in separate realities.

There were two terrible things about dying. One was the waiting. Sometimes she would feel herself drawn into sleep, and she would make peace with herself one more time, knowing she wouldn't waken, and then she would. Sometimes she would lie there, gigantic eyeballs closed, and wonder if she was dead or alive, not really being able to tell. And then Peter would move, or she would activate those heavy eyelids, and she would see, dimly, that she still breathed, her skin still crawled, something still twitched.

The other terrible thing about dying was the falling. It was one thing that made her maybe not want to die. She would be sliding into sleep—or death, as the case may be—and dream she was falling, and jerk herself violently awake. Each time it happened, her poor skinny heart worked overtime, and she would say to herself, "Next time, I'll just go. I'll just fall into that death and not let this wretched body baggage pull me back."

But she always jerked herself back. Ten, twelve times a day, she would startle herself back.

And when her mind wasn't occupied with a thousand

other aspects of this serious business of dying, she tried to think up profound last words to say to Peter.

She would do well to be rid of Peter. She didn't even want to see him on The Other Side.

And then one day, after startling herself awake, she remembered the story about a man in the old west who made his living by carrying a rattlesnake around in a big jar. He'd go into the saloons and bet the locals that they couldn't hold their hand up to the glass and keep it there while the snake struck. Their pride made them try it again and again, whole barsful of egotistical men, and of course, nothing could keep the instinctive recoil of their hands from the glass as that snake struck, its venom leaking down the inside of the bottle.

That's all this is, she thought, this startling awake all the time. I'm just recoiling from the snake. I'm not afraid. I'm not going to do it anymore.

She closed her eyes and dropped right through.

* * *

Peter knew exactly when Tess died. He heard her sigh. It had been coming, they both knew it, but the reality of it still shook him.

He didn't have the twitches the way she did, but the absence of those twitching muscles in the bed next to him left him more solidly alone than at any other time in his life.

Peter felt his bones hollowing out. With every rasping breath, he could feel the little blades scraping, scraping on the insides of his bones. As long as Tess was beside him, he could tolerate it, he could lie on that mattress that had become a cesspool in their weakness, and try to communicate with whatever tiny beings wielded those tiny knives.

But when Tess died, Peter came aware with a sudden surge of desperation. It was as if he awakened from a long, dark, disturbing dream.

A knocking came at the door. And then yelling.

"Hey, you. You weirdos. You in there? Something's stinking up the place. Is it you guys? Answer the door, you idiot fuckheads, or I'll call the super."

Peter would have opened the door, but he could no longer get out of bed. Just thinking about it made him weaker. He had little breath left, his lungs worked overtime to take a shallow gulp of air. The last time he spoke, he had to breathe between each word, and even now he lay panting, hoping the people would break down the door, come in and take him to a hospital.

He must have been insane. He knew Tess had been. She was the one. She had been crazy, and now she was dead, and he needed to be rescued before it was too late.

"She killed my father," he whispered, but whoever had been at the door was gone.

There was food and drink in Tess's drawer. Peter thought about it for a long time. If he could get over there, could he get the beer bottle open?

He tried to visualize turning over, climbing over Tess, opening her drawer. In his mind's eye, he could see mouse droppings in the bottom of the drawer instead of the cookies he knew she had left in there. They'd both heard the mice.

But there was one beer left in there, he knew it.

His tongue swelled at the thought. His saliva grew thick and sour.

But to move—

The thought of movement made his reconstructed hip joint grind as if it were filled with grit.

Oh, but that beer.

Very slowly, Peter leaned up on one elbow and waited while dizziness and nausea faded. His hip screamed. He rolled over onto his stomach and wrestled his arm out from underneath him. If he rolled over again, Tess would be under his back and he'd be facing up, trying to get into her nightstand. Instead, he crawled up over her torso. He rested a minute on top of her.

She was cold. And thin. Her cheekbones showed shiny through the slight layer of skin covering them. She was ugly.

"I'm glad you're dead," he whispered, and the coughing took him.

When he was finished coughing, there was a clump of red tissue on Tess's chest. He'd never seen that before. He brought a hand up to his mouth and it came away bloody.

He relaxed, just for a moment, and found that tears pulsed, ready to flow. The trek across the bed was too much for the tennis pro. He had fallen into Tess's Candyland and now he would never leave. Never have children, grandchildren, never taste another steak, never enjoy another slow, comfortable screw.

He gagged, then coughed, and rich red blood flowed out

of is mouth onto Tess's chest, ran off the sheet and pooled beneath them.

It's too late for that beer, he thought.

He heard someone at the door. Knocking. Pounding. Yelling. He tried to swallow, not wanting to swallow too much blood, but it was gushing now, and there was no stopping it. His lungs were filling. They felt extraordinarily heavy. He resisted the urge to cough.

Then he did cough, and blood sprayed Tess's face and the wall behind her.

My God, Peter thought, then put his head down on her chest again.

I did love you once, Tess, he thought. I did believe in Candyland.

The superintendent opened the door with a key, and while the men were dealing with the sight of Peter's father on the kitchen floor, Peter quietly died.

EPILOGUE
NOVEMBER

All three of the bodies were easily identified. Depositions were taken from the neighbors, the deli delivery boy, the business office who paid the bills, and Tess' ex-husband, Charles.

What confounded Detective Anderson, the investigating officer most, was the abundance of written gibberish that lay strewn about the bedroom. Papers were folded into tiny squares and inserted into all manner of cracks and crevices. Dozens of spiral-bound notebooks were filled with small, cramped writing, even one pillowcase was covered with the stuff.

He gathered up all of the pages, including the ones with the drawings, and took them home, where he searched for meaning, for a clue to the encryption.

Eventually, he lost interest, and while he thought for a while of having a cryptologist look over the stuff—Jesus Christ, there had to be some kind of an explanation for what those people did to themselves!—he could not afford it personally, and neither could the department. Besides, the department wasn't interested.

One cold day, his son wadded up some of the sheets to start a fire in the fireplace.

At first, the detective was horrified. This was the journal of somebody's life!

And yet, they were dead; they lived a terrible life, they died a terrible death—who wanted to revive all kinds of sick bullshit? It was just as well. He took the pile of papers and notebooks into the living room and set them by the fireplace to be used with the kindling.

Then he pulled his young son close to him, loving the feel of the flesh of his flesh, and they rocked together, watching the fire, watching the wadded papers burn. He ruffled his boy's hair, and began to dream of the boy's future. He had great potential, this kid. And it was a father's duty to make sure the kid lived up to his potential.

And he would, by god. He would remember this moment, and he would remember those sad sick folks in that horrible apartment, and he would make damned sure that his kid had a good life, a successful life, a better life than he had had as a mediocre husband and provider, father and cop.

His son would live the better life, and as a father, he'd make damned sure of it.

ABOUT THE AUTHOR

Elizabeth Engstrom is the author of sixteen internationally-acclaimed books and well over 250 short stories, articles and essays. Her most recent work of fiction is a Labyrinth of Souls novel, *Benediction Denied*, a descent into darkness and madness. Her most recent nonfiction book is *How to Write a Sizzling Sex Scene*. This novel *Candyland* was recently made into Candiland, a major motion picture starring Gary Busey, Chelah Horsdal and James Clayton. Engstrom is a sought-after panelist, keynote speaker, and instructor at writing conferences and conventions around the world. She lives in the Pacific Northwest with her fisherman-husband and puts her pen to work for social justice. She is always working on the next book.
www.elizabethengstrom.com

IFD Publishing Paperbacks

Novels:

Death is a Star, by Christina Lay
Baggage Check, by Elizabeth Engstrom
Bull's Labyrinth, by Eric Witchey
The Surgeon's Mate: A Dismemoir, by Alan M. Clark
Siren Promised, by Jeremy Robert Johnson and Alan M. Clark
Say Anything but Your Prayers, by Alan M. Clark
Candyland, by Elizabeth Engstrom
Apologies to the Cat's Meat Man, by Alan M. Clark

Collections:

Professor Witchey's Miracle Mood Cure, by Eric Witchey

Nonfiction:

How to Write a Sizzling Sex Scene by Elizabeth Engstrom

IFD Publishing EBooks

(You can find the following titles at most distribution points for all ereading platforms.)

Novels:

Bull's Labyrinth, by Eric Witchey
The Surgeon's Mate: A Dismemoir, by Alan M. Clark
York's Moon, by Elizabeth Engstrom
Beyond the Serpent's Heart, by Eric Witchey
Lizzie Borden, by Elizabeth Engstrom
A Parliament of Crows, by Alan M. Clark
Lizard Wine, by Elizabeth Engstrom
Northwoods Chronicles: A Novel in Short Stories, by Elizabeth Engstrom
Siren Promised, by Alan M. Clark and Jeremy Robert Johnson
To Kill a Common Loon, by Mitch Luckett
The Man in the Loon, by Mitch Luckett
Jack the Ripper Victim Series: Of Thimble and Threat by Alan M. Clark

Jack the Ripper Victim Series: The Double Event (includes two novels from the series: *Of Thimble and Threat* and *Say Anything But Your Prayers*) by Alan M. Clark
Candyland, by Elizabeth Engstrom
The Blood of Father Time: Book 1, The New Cut, by Alan M. Clark, Stephen C. Merritt & Lorelei Shannon
The Blood of Father Time: Book 2, The Mystic Clan's Grand Plot, by Alan M. Clark, Stephen C. Merritt & Lorelei Shannon
How I Met My Alien Bitch Lover: Book 1 from the Sunny World Inquisition Daily Letter Archives, by Eric Witchey
Baggage Check, by Elizabeth Engstrom
Death is a Star, by Christina Lay
D. D. Murphy, Secret Policeman, by Alan M. Clark and Elizabeth Massie
Black Leather, by Elizabeth Engstrom

Novelettes:
The Tao of Flynn, by Eric Witchey
To Build a Boat, Listen to Trees, by Eric Witchey

Children's Illustrated:
The Christmas Thingy, by F. Paul Wilson. Illustrated by Alan M. Clark

Collections:
Suspicions, by Elizabeth Engstrom
Professor Witchey's Miracle Mood Cure, by Eric Witchey

Short Fiction:
"Brittle Bones and Old Rope," by Alan M. Clark
"Crosley," by Elizabeth Engstrom
"The Apple Sniper," by Eric Witchey

Nonfiction:
How to Write a Sizzling Sex Scene by Elizabeth Engstrom

IFD Publishing Audio Books

Novels:

The Door That Faced West by Alan M. Clark, read by Charles Hinckley

Jack the Ripper Victim Series: Of Thimble and Threat by Alan M. Clark, read by Alicia Rose

Jack the Ripper Victim Series: Say Anything But Your Prayers by Alan M. Clark, read by Alicia Rose

Jack the Ripper Victim Series: The Double Event by Alan M. Clark, read by Alicia Rose (includes two novels from the series: *Of Thimble and Threat* and *Say Anything But Your Prayers*)

A Parliament of Crows by Alan M. Clark, read by Laura Jennings

A Brutal Chill in August by Alan M. Clark, read by Alicia Rose

The Surgeon's Mate: A Dismemoir by Alan M. Clark, read by Alan M. Clark

CPSIA information can be obtained
at www.ICGtesting.com
Printed in the USA
LVOW12s0420290417
532640LV00001BA/216/P